Books by Crissy Smith

I0546046

Pack Mates

ISBN # 978-1-78686-310-2

©Copyright Crissy Smith 2017

Cover Art by Posh Gosh ©Copyright 2017

Interior text design by Claire Siemaszkiewicz

Totally Bound Publishing

Were Chronicles

PACK MATES

CRISSY SMITH

Dedication

For the fans, who have waited — and begged — for the Were Chronicles to continue.

Chapter One

It was late March and already the temperature had hit over ninety degrees in south-east New Mexico. Nikki Stratton groaned as the air conditioner in her old Jeep barely managed to cool the interior of the vehicle.

Thirty-two years old and she'd been called home like a teenager. She resented the fact that she'd let her older brothers demand her appearance and was still disgusted with herself for not having put up a fight.

She continued to speed down the interstate toward her home town, both dread and anxiety sitting in her stomach. A new Alpha had been named for her Pack. Since she still maintained Pack status, she'd been beckoned home to welcome him and the new members he'd brought to join their family. That was what she supposed, anyway. Brandon hadn't actually *told* her why he wanted her home. He'd just stated she needed to leave the next day. Justin, the middle sibling, hadn't given any hint, either—had just told her the new Alpha would take over this week and she needed to come home.

It wasn't even that she didn't want to be there. She'd planned to take some vacation time and visit her siblings soon, but being ordered home left her feeling like a cub again. She loved her brothers, but sometimes they put the needs of the Pack ahead of their immediate family.

Her oldest brother, Brandon, worked as both the town sheriff and enforcer of the Pack. Her other brother, Justin, was a teacher, in public and in Pack life, too. Their wants and needs had been built around being able to serve their fellow wolves. Nikki just hadn't been born that way. She liked to be free, to travel and to be on her own. Unusual for a wolf, yes, but not unheard of. Away from home, she'd not only met other wolves who felt like she did, but other shifters, too—felines, birds and even a very nice shifter bear family. Nikki felt more at home with them sometimes than with her old Pack.

Her family had never understood her independence, but at least they'd always supported her. She'd been lucky and couldn't bitch too much about it. And she began to feel guilty and just a little childish about her feelings. Except... she liked her life. Now she worried that her carefully constructed way of living was about to change. Why else would she have to come home, with no choice in the matter? Brandon had never asked that of her.

The exit sign for their town came up and Nikki had to fight the urge to keep driving. She slowed to make the curved side road that would take her straight into downtown Lawton, a small, private cotton and farming community.

Little had changed in the year and a half she'd been away. She'd gone to the big city of Houston, Texas, at nineteen to attend college and had never returned. Oh, sure, she'd made certain that she returned every few years or so, but only to visit her brothers. Nikki was different from many of the others she'd grown up with. Instead of craving a mate and children, she was looking for excitement. She wasn't ready to settle down quite yet. And living in Lawton would ensure that would happen.

The county line WELCOME sign drew a sigh from her. She felt like a different person in Lawton. Always having to defend her nomadic ways.

If she were as honest as possible, it felt good to know that she always had a place to return to. Yes, even if she never said it out loud, sometimes she missed her family.

Nikki let up off the gas pedal even more to drive in at the posted thirty-five miles per hour. She wouldn't put it past Brandon to pull her over and ticket her if he caught her speeding. She chuckled to herself—it had, in fact, happened many times.

The library was closed already, reminding her that at six on a Sunday night, she wouldn't have to worry about running into too many people. The café was open and had a half-full parking lot. But the other buildings—post office, salon, thrift store—were dark and locked up tight. Lights blazed to the right. Of course, the sheriff's office stayed open twenty-four hours a day. Not that there was a lot of crime, but put a group of secretive wolf shifters in a community and there were bound to be several paranoid people. She happened to be related to one.

As if her thoughts had brought him out, the front door of the sheriff's office opened and Brandon stepped through.

His dark brown hair looked to be several weeks past a trim and reached over his ears. His strong muscular shoulders and arms bulged from his khaki uniform shirt, while his long legs ate up the ground as he made his way to the street. He turned and his green eyes flashed as he spotted her vehicle. The grin he sent her was so much better than the pictures she carried that she couldn't help but smile back.

He wrenched the door to her Jeep open before she'd even cut the engine. She slammed it into Park and turned the key right and he pulled her out and into his arms.

"Hey, sister," he greeted her, squeezing tight.

"Bran!" she managed to squeak out.

He chuckled then set her on her feet. "Let me look at you." He did the customary check she went through every time she came home. He ran his hands over her head, down her hair to her face, coming to a final rest on her shoulders.

He nodded. "You need to eat more, but you look good."

Nikki rolled her eyes. She hadn't expected him to say anything different.

Brandon grinned and threw an arm around her neck, yanking her close once again. "I was just headed to meet Justin for a bite. Now you can join me."

She groaned. After driving for a day and a half, all she

wanted was to rest.

"Oh, don't complain. You need to eat. Then Justin can grab a ride home with you instead of waiting on me." He slammed her vehicle door closed then led her away. It didn't escape her notice that he didn't lock it up — something she could never forget to do in Houston.

"Fine." She let herself be dragged down the street, heading to the café she'd passed on her way into town. The stores she passed were new. Lawton now had a flower shop, tattoo parlor and dry cleaners. "New businesses?" There hadn't been any of those shops in the entire time she'd grown up there. No one had ever moved there to open a business.

"Cameron started working with the new Alpha to bring his Pack members here before he stepped down. Cam wants us to be comfortable and see the plus side of adding to the Pack," Brandon explained.

"How many shifters did we add?"

"Over fifty."

She gasped. In a matter of a few months, the Pack size had doubled.

"It's a good thing." Brandon responded to her reaction. "Offered jobs to those in the Pack who needed them."

He'd said that with more feeling than normal. Either he was still trying to convince himself or there were already problems. She'd have to talk to Justin about it later. Justin didn't usually try to keep her out of what was happening, thinking he'd protect her, like Brandon always did. Not all the time, anyway. Her brothers couldn't help it. Brandon had raised his two younger siblings since he'd been barely an adult. Their father had left them as soon as he felt they'd been old enough to be on their own. The loss of his mate had been just too much for him to live with.

She wanted to remember good times with her parents but as she'd gotten older, she found it harder and harder to bring up those memories. Brandon had been the one who'd attended her parent-teacher conferences. Brandon had bought Nikki her first pair of soccer shoes and later her first camera. Her older brother had been the dad she'd needed more than her real old man had ever been.

After having left home, Nikki had come to understand everything that Brandon had sacrificed for her and Justin. And thinking about this made the guilt from earlier return. Nikki needed to give Brandon a break. She knew that, but sometimes her brother frustrated her.

Just as they reached the door to the café, she was greeted with a shriek and yanked into the arms of another woman. Chuckling and glad she still remembered the scent of her best friend from childhood, Sabrina, she grinned, hugging back.

"Nik!" Sabrina held her close.

"Hey there, honey," she greeted. "It's good to see you." Nikki meant the words, too. Part of leaving Lawton had meant not only being away from her brothers but also the friends who were just like family as well.

"I can't believe you're here. I was just saying the other day that you haven't come to visit in forever. You haven't even met little Julian yet."

Since she was still being squashed, she gently tried to extract herself from her friend. Sabrina didn't seem to want to let go.

"Baby, give her room to breathe or you're gonna make her pass out," Sabrina's mate, Max, said, coming to her rescue and pulling her friend from her.

Sabrina laughed. "All right."

Nikki smiled over at her friend. Sabrina had grown to be such a lovely woman. Short-cropped blonde hair, styled and sassy, fit her petite frame and her quirky personality. But it was the glow in Sabrina that warmed Nikki's heart. She looked so happy.

"We have to catch up. Oh, we have so much to talk about," Sabrina said grabbing Nikki's hands.

"Oh, yes, and I'll finally get to meet baby Julian and see Jesse and Jeremy," Nikki agreed. She still talked to her oldest friend as much as she could, but with two busy lives, work, family and everything else, it had been too long. "Why don't you bring the kids over for breakfast in the morning?"

"A breakfast cooked by someone else?" Sabrina asked with a smile. "We are so there."

Nikki nodded and pulled her friend in for another hug. "Eight o'clock — don't be late."

Sabrina agreed then let her mate lead her across the parking lot.

"She looks so great," Nikki told her brother.

"She's happy," he answered. "But I want to know why you're not making your favorite brother breakfast?"

She slapped his stomach then pulled the door open. "Justin can eat if he wants to."

Brandon growled and reached for her. She laughed and jumped out of the way, bumping into someone.

"Oh, sorry," she murmured, peering up. And up. She was forced to tilt her head back to see the man in front of her.

"No problem at all," he responded in a deep rumble that vibrated the air around her.

Her breath caught as she stared up at the man. Dark, almost black hair hung over his dark eyes. His lips tilted up at the edges in a small smile while he moved to the side. She didn't even realize she had stepped closer until Brandon touched her lower back, breaking her attention on the stranger.

"RJ." Brandon greeted the stranger. Nikki didn't miss the tension in her brother's body or his tone.

"Good evening, Sheriff." The man nodded. "Ma'am."

Nikki snorted. *"Ma'am?"*

Amusement shined in the stranger's gaze. "Well, if I knew your name..."

"It's Nikki Stratton," she informed him, holding out her hand. She wasn't worried about Brandon's cold greeting. Her older brother's protectiveness had always had him growling at her dates. This man deserved a real introduction instead of the shortness of her brother. "You must be new to town."

He took it and winked. Electricity sizzled from her fingertips up her arm. She'd become locked into that dark gaze and her body tingled with need. His dark eyes had a sparkle to them. "RJ Cross. I haven't seen you around here. Visiting?"

"You could say that," she replied. Nikki was still a registered Pack member, so she wouldn't call her coming home a visit, but she didn't mind the flirting. "Although I do know all the good places around here, if you need a tour guide."

"Is that so?" RJ's grin remained wicked.

Damn, maybe I can ditch my brothers and –

"Now that everyone's met, can we go eat?" Brandon snapped from beside her.

She sighed and removed her hand from RJ's hold. *Okay, maybe I can't bail on dinner, but I'll certainly go find Mister Tall, Dark and Handsome again.* "Well, I guess I'll be seeing you around town," she flirted with the stranger. She really, *really* wanted to see him again.

"Oh, I can almost guarantee it." RJ looked over to Brandon and nodded. The smile was no longer present and the chill grew between the two men.

Interesting. Brandon usually didn't allow his job to interfere out in public, but she got the feeling that he and RJ had had a few run-ins.

"Sheriff," RJ said, while already walking away.

His spectacular ass in a pair of tight, worn blue jeans kept her attention until Brandon tugged on her arm. Nikki allowed herself to be manhandled into the café.

"Who's that?" she asked once they'd stepped inside.

"Trouble," Brandon replied. "You don't want to get involved with him."

"Get involved with who?"

Nikki turned to Justin and jumped into his arms. Justin, of course, embraced her, only stumbling a little. "Hey, bro," Nikki said.

"Hi, so who were you checking out?"

"No one," Brandon interrupted. "Do we have a table?"

Justin raised an eyebrow at her before giving his winning smile to the oldest Stratton. "Over here," he said, guiding her toward the back.

Nikki was surprised to see the old restaurant almost packed to capacity. There weren't a lot of places to eat out in town, but almost everyone cooked their own meals. Even more shocking were the number of new faces she didn't recognize. Several people waved and called out a greeting as she passed.

There was definitely something going on that she didn't know about.

Justin pointed to a booth and she slid in, with him following close behind. Nikki glanced up and saw that several old men at one table had stopped Brandon to talk. It wasn't like the sheriff's office wasn't right across the street. They could talk to Brandon anytime, but by the looks of things, they had plenty to say.

"What's that about?" Nikki nodded toward the group.

Justin picked up a menu and passed it to her. "There are a couple new dishes you might want to try."

The non-answer was not a good sign.

"Justin?"

"Let it go." Her brother peered around. "There'll be plenty of time to talk, but here's not the place or time."

So he knew why Brandon had wanted her home. "Fine." The menu had indeed been updated. It seemed like the White family had at last listened to the residents' complaints. Nikki had always believed that the only reason the café was still in business was because of lack of choices. "This doesn't look so bad."

"New Pack members brought in some business. There's now a bakery and coffee shop plus a family style restaurant. The Whites had to step up or lose their business," Justin told her.

Nikki glanced around the crowded area. "It worked."

Justin snorted. "This isn't because of the food."

"What's that mean?" she whispered, leaning closer to Justin.

"But who's here?" Justin advised. "All the busybodies of the Pack."

That was true. While she received warm greetings from several of the Pack, she also received glares from a few of the older women. The ones who'd told Brandon that she shouldn't be going off to college.

Brandon straightened before heading toward their table. Justin picked up his menu, hiding his face. Nikki guessed she'd have to wait to get him alone to grill him further.

"Order whatever you want," Brandon said as he sat. "You're too thin."

Nikki rolled her eyes. She was in fact at a normal range on the weight scale. It wasn't easy for a shifter to gain weight, anyway. Still, the complaint was common and, as she'd done in the past, she'd just ignore her oldest brother.

"So, Brandon," she said. "How're things going here?"

He glanced up at her for a second before peering around. "Fine."

Okay, so she needed another topic — something safer.

"How's the crime in town? Bust any bank robbers or million-dollar theft rings?" Nikki joked.

Brandon grunted as Justin folded his menu, sighing.

Damn. Nikki was running out of ideas on what they could discuss. Luckily, the waitress approached their table. Nikki wanted to get the meal out of the way as soon as possible, so she could find out what was going on.

RJ Cross turned to catch the final sight of the young woman until she disappeared to the back of the café behind her brother. The smile fell from his face once she walked out of sight. Without question, she was one of the most gorgeous women he'd ever laid eyes on. Her long dark hair had been streaked with blonde, which added an attractive touch. Her green eyes had sparkled and her slender body was just to his liking. But her being a Stratton was an added complication. He and Brandon Stratton hadn't started off on the best of terms. In fact, the more he was around the sheriff, the less RJ liked him. Brandon had an attitude toward his entire family. RJ shook his head and started down the street to his shop.

His youngest brother had worked hard, getting RJ's tattoo store front set up while RJ had been on his last mission. As he stood in front of the tinted windows with their scrawling script, he couldn't help the pride that flooded him.

Finally, after years of serving his country and fighting for other people's needs, RJ had a place that he could call all his own.

Being part of an exclusive shifter military unit hadn't been bad. He still kept in close contact to the men he considered family, but the wolf shifter in him wanted to settle down and claim his own spot. RJ had done just that, joining his brothers in Lawton. Even if their welcome hadn't been quite smooth, RJ was now home.

Instead of going inside, he walked to the rear where he had his Harley parked. The alley looked as clean as it had been that morning when he'd arrived, but RJ still took his time scenting the area. No one had been by. *Good.* He was more than likely being over-cautious, but until things around the town became more welcoming, RJ would need to be prepared for danger.

All three Cross brothers were making the rounds, trying to get to know the established Pack members, but RJ had his suspicions. He didn't think the additional Pack was in for that smooth a transition.

One of the reasons he'd decided to stop at the café on his way home had been to show his face, make his presence felt. Now he was glad he had done. Running into Nikki Stratton had been a pleasant twist to the already long day. She hadn't reacted the way most of the townsfolk had. If he had to guess, RJ would say that she'd not known he was part of the inner circle that had been brought into her Pack.

Oh, I'm sure she'll find out soon enough. Brandon Stratton would for sure inform his sister just who RJ was.

He climbed on his bike and started it up. The rumble and vibration under him felt good and he took off toward the main street. It was already quiet on the road that would lead him home. No other vehicles were out and most of the residents were behind the doors of their own houses.

The small community he'd moved to with his Pack was a pretty piece of America. The Pack had come from the mountains of Colorado, and he'd worried that his family and Pack members wouldn't adjust well. The last eight years had kept him away more than he'd liked, but both his brothers had filled him in on Pack life every time RJ had called home. He might have been away, but RJ had never abandoned his family. Now he had as many new members as he had old. It would be interesting to see how the two Packs came together — if they ever did. Not exactly how RJ wanted to start his civilian life, but when Dylan had called, RJ couldn't have said no.

His older brother had asked for him to come help him lead a new Pack and RJ had known it had been time. He'd met some great people along the way, but he'd wanted to see his family more. To be a part of something else.

The members of the Pack who had followed Dylan loved the town. Some had even made new friendships. RJ's relationship with the incoming Alpha appeared to be what was keeping him under constant scrutiny. Even though he and Dylan were clearly very different men, the residents of Lawton were still unsure whether RJ belonged as well. He didn't know anything but time that would help. That and when Dylan became Alpha, the Pack seeing Dylan as the good man and great leader he'd be.

The quick ride to the house he stayed at with his brothers ended, and he thought about riding around for a little longer. He enjoyed driving the long, empty roads throughout the territory, but he had business to take care of. Dylan would need an update on what RJ had learned. No doubt Dylan waited for him. RJ parked under the carport between the two trucks that had beaten him home. The lights were on in the front windows as he made his way across the wood porch. He let himself in, being greeted by the coolness of the air and the sound of a ball game on the television in the den.

Home. He could now come home to the house with his family instead of a sleeping bag in the dirt, like he'd spent so many long nights. RJ followed the noise to the doorway where he found his two brothers. Dylan was lounging in one of the leather chairs, legs spread as he slouched, drinking a beer. RJ's younger brother had his head buried in a book sitting on one side of the large couch. He ruffled his 'little' sibling's hair as he stepped beside him and dropped down next to him.

"Hey!" Ben grumbled, not looking up from his book.

RJ grinned meeting Dylan's gaze. Ben hadn't been much more than a lanky teenager when RJ had enlisted in the military. RJ had missed his brother becoming an adult. There had been more than a little relief that Ben remained the same kind-hearted, gentle and brilliant young man RJ hadn't gotten to see a lot of.

Dylan smiled and shook his head. "How'd work go?"

RJ just shrugged. Opening a tattoo shop in a small town might not be very profitable, but he enjoyed his art and, in point of fact, didn't need the money anyway. "Had a couple people drop by, but no new customers. I think they wanted to check out the new Alpha's brother more than any art."

Dylan nodded. "Give them time. The town will open up to us."

The way Dylan said the words, so certain, helped ease some of RJ's stress. RJ hoped Dylan was right, but that wasn't his biggest concern. "I stopped by the café tonight."

Dylan must have caught something in his tone, because he switched the game to mute and sat up straighter.

"I overhead two men talking about the ceremony," RJ told him.

Beside him, Ben put his book down and turned toward him. Now he had both their attentions.

"They suggested there might be a challenge after the ceremony."

Dylan sat back and RJ let the man think. The rumors about a challenge had started to build in the last few weeks. Now, just days prior to the ceremony, they had picked up even more. It had always been a possibility when Cameron King had asked Dylan to take over as Alpha that a challenge would come from someone who wanted the top position.

There were only two ways to become an Alpha of a Pack – to be appointed or to challenge the standing Alpha. Cameron King was an honest, kind and well-respected Alpha. Dylan was new to the territory. An unknown. "What bothers me the most is that the men talking had to know I'd overhear them. It's like they didn't care."

"Any idea who'd issue the challenge?" Dylan asked, in concern.

RJ ran his hands over his face. This was the tricky part. He didn't want to add to the gossip, but he had to protect his brother. "Talk is Brandon Stratton."

Dylan didn't look surprised. "I thought it would be. He's the wolf closest to matching my strength. Cameron did tell me he spoke with Brandon when he started to think about stepping down. Let him know about me."

RJ waited for his brother to continue.

"At the time Brandon didn't want the position. Said he wasn't born to lead and knew it."

"Doesn't mean he hasn't changed his mind." Ben spoke up for the first time.

Smaller than his two brothers, Ben Cross stayed the quiet and peaceful one. He'd been born with the ability to calm those around him. It was what made him such a good diplomat for the Pack.

"Yeah, it's one thing to not want to be Alpha and another to have someone else come in and take over," Dylan agreed.

"The thing is," RJ said, "Brandon might not like it, but I

don't get the feeling he's planning on challenging you. He hasn't exactly welcomed me, but he doesn't go out of his way to make up conflict. Other than the argument when I first reached town, he's been somewhat civil. He doesn't like me, but I think that has more to do with him thinking I'm some kind of asshole biker."

"You *are* an asshole biker," Ben commented.

"True." RJ nodded then reached over and cuffed the back of Ben's head. "But you don't have to point it out."

"Ow." Ben frowned at him. "Maybe Brandon doesn't want to be Alpha, but he's being pressured. I could see how that might be making him uncomfortable."

All three of them sat in silence, thinking their own thoughts for several minutes, before Dylan spoke again.

"Well, there's nothing we can do until the challenge is issued. Just keep an ear out."

RJ tilted his head in agreement. They had to wait. Nothing more to do, according to his brother. He might not like it, but it was Dylan's call. At least on the outside. What RJ found out on his own didn't have to affect Dylan one way or another. "I'm going to head up to shower."

Ben picked his book up and sent him a wave of his hand, but Dylan still stared at him. "Is that all?" Dylan asked, his tone low.

RJ didn't know how he did it. Dylan could tell when something was going on with one of them. He thought about telling him about Nikki but didn't want to add to his brother's worries. And maybe he wanted to keep her a secret just a little bit longer. He could still smell the citrus from her shampoo, feel the softness of her hand in his, and wanted to enjoy the moment before he had to deal with the tension between the two families.

"For now," he answered his brother, keeping things vague.

"I'm here if you need me," Dylan told him; reaching for the remote again.

RJ headed up the stairs to the first room down the hall. He

liked being closest to the stairs in case of problems during the night. He had served as an Enforcer in his Pack as well as the specialized military unit he'd been assigned to. But after his latest mission to protect the feline Prince and the battle once he'd been rescued, RJ had needed some time off. Dylan's call had been a welcome excuse to make the changes that he'd been thinking about for several months. He wasn't the only one who'd been ready to leave. Luckily, the others in their unit had also made plans for their futures.

The first time that Dylan had told RJ about the opportunity in Lawton, RJ had been filled with a sense of pride in his brother.

Everyone could tell that Dylan had been born a natural leader, and when their Alpha had heard that Cameron King wanted to retire, he had suggested a meeting between the two men. Their Alpha, Craig, was a good man and had several sons who would be able to lead their Pack into the future. Dylan would never have challenged them if they ran the Pack with a fair hand and Craig knew it. Craig had been offered a position on the Alpha council and, as any good leader would, had suggested some changes. One of them had been for Dylan and Cameron to meet, Craig believing that Dylan should get the chance to lead his own Pack.

So Craig had urged Dylan to meet with Cameron and had even talked several others into joining the Pack Dylan would lead. More had come than any of them had thought. Craig had understood and encouraged them all. He wanted his Pack members to flourish, but with over two hundred shifters under his command, he knew there were some wolves who couldn't reach their potential in such a large group.

Moving to the new territory had been a great opportunity for them all.

His room was dark and cool as he pushed the door open. He'd brought his furniture from the childhood home they'd lived in all their lives. He missed the old house, but having something to remind him of his past helped. He had a small apartment above his shop in town, but he had yet to do more than move in a couch, futon and odds and ends. It was convenient if he worked late or needed to grab a shower, but he liked being close with his brothers. Plus, until he knew all threat to Dylan had passed, he would be here.

He tried to picture Nikki there with him in his bedroom, which might have been a little ridiculous since he'd just met the woman, but it had been a long time since anyone had grabbed RJ's attention. Even in his downtime, RJ was always with his unit. Their bonds ran deep.

At first sight, Nikki had woken that part of him that had seemed to have gone to sleep. Hell, his cock was still hard from just the brief touch of her hand in his.

He'd love to see how the rest of her body felt under him. His room, surrounded by the familiar scents of home, would be perfect. Would she find it too masculine, or would she see the beauty of the stained wood the way he did? The large four-poster bed dominated most of the north wall. He was a tall man at six-foot-five. He liked to have plenty of room to sprawl out. He could just see her spread for him in the middle of the bed. Legs open and inviting, arms stretched above her head, her body arching in need.

He yanked his black T-shirt over his head and dropped it to the floor before he sat on the edge of the bed and pulled off his boots and socks. The desire he had clearly read when he'd locked gazes with her had tempted his control. And just the one slight touch they'd briefly shared had sent his blood boiling.

There'd be a lot that he could imagine doing with her. Like how soft her skin would be as he caressed and teased her toward pleasure. The moans and gasps he'd be able to swallow from her lips. Damn, just the images were enough to make him need to blow.

RJ stood but couldn't resist dropping his fingers low to play with the zipper on his jeans. He wanted more than just her hands, though. Her mouth, with her easy smile, had been made for pleasuring a man. He groaned as he pictured her on her knees in front of him. *Oh, yeah.* He could almost feel the warm, wet tongue tracing his balls then sucking him in.

"Fuck." He ripped off his jeans to stand stark naked, panting with need. He licked his palm then started to stroke himself, each rough tug drawing him closer to completion. It had just been his hand for too long, and now that he'd found a woman who called to both the man and wolf, he was ready to explode in an instant. RJ concentrated on each detail of Nikki Stratton as he urgently played with himself. Oh, he couldn't wait to mark her with his mouth, his teeth and his cum. Bend her over the bed and pound into her while sinking his canines into the base of her neck.

The last fantasy sent him over the edge. His seed shot out as he pumped his cock and he almost collapsed at the intensity of his orgasm.

He dropped on the bed and smiled.

Complications be damned. RJ had something to look forward to. He'd need to learn more about her and why she'd all of a sudden shown up in town. That would give him time to ensure that he had complete control of the urges she wrenched from him.

If Nikki had come there to help her brother hurt Dylan or any of the Pack, he needed to find out. No matter how much he wanted the sexy shifter.

Chapter Two

Nikki had enjoyed dinner with her two brothers, mostly because of how much she'd missed them. Maybe it was just what she did to convince herself that she was okay on her own, but the loneliness of not being part of their stories actually hurt.

Justin had delighted her with the antics of both his second-grade class and the pre-teen wolves he taught. Brandon had remained quiet throughout most of the meal, which wasn't out of the ordinary, but she'd picked up his tension anyhow. Something big was going on and they'd been keeping her in the dark about it. The little she'd gotten out of Justin wasn't enough.

She bided her time until Brandon headed for the station and Justin was sitting in the passenger seat of her Jeep. Justin wouldn't be able to get out of her questioning that way.

"What's going on?" she asked, turning south off the main street to where their small home was. "What haven't I been told?"

Justin sighed gazing out of the window. "The ceremony in a few days is getting people worked up. Brandon needs you here."

"Why?" She darted a look at him, but he still faced away. "It's not like we didn't know it's going to happen." Brandon had called and said Cameron was stepping down. He had explained about the new Alpha coming and how their community would grow.

"Yeah, but knowing and it actually happening are two different things."

"So Brandon wanted me home to show support for the change or something?" Normally Justin was a lot easier to get answers from. "Have you met the new Alpha?"

"Once. He seemed like a good enough guy," Justin admitted. "But he's not from here."

"Well, Cameron has already picked the Alpha and it's been agreed upon by the council," she reminded him. "What is there to do?"

"The new Alpha could be challenged right after the ceremony."

Her hands jerked and the vehicle swerved. She righted the steering wheel. "Shit—a challenge?"

She'd never seen a challenge but knew enough about them to know that a battle for the position for Alpha would be major. Some of her friends had told her stories about the Pack being taken over. The Alpha who lost never lived. Although the Council tried to keep the chance of death minimal, there were old-fashioned Alphas who still demanded it.

This was much worse than Nikki had expected. *Good thing I've come home.* If Brandon was going to protect the new Alpha… A sudden thought entered her brain. "Who would be stupid enough to challenge the Alpha?" she asked.

When Justin simply turned and met her stare, she knew.

"Oh, God! He can't!"

Justin just shrugged. "I don't think he even wants to. But he's getting a lot of pressure right now. I don't know what he's going to do, but a day doesn't go by that someone is not calling or coming by to ask him about it."

And suddenly she understood. She wasn't home just to welcome the new Alpha. She might be saying goodbye to her own brother. A challenge to the death. Or even if the new Alpha decided to spare Brandon's life, he'd have to leave the Pack. She and Justin would have to leave the only home they'd ever had.

Tears pricked her eyes as she peered out of the windshield. The sights that surrounded her were so familiar, but they didn't soothe her like they normally did. Now, they made her feel sick. They'd lived there since her grandfather had joined the small community and had brought his young mate with him. Her grandmother's family had been part of the territory for several decades. The wide-open space that expanded for miles and miles was home. But *home* also meant family. Her family, Brandon and Justin, all she had left.

"We can't let him," she almost yelled in the small, quiet confines of the vehicle.

"We don't have a choice. If he decides to do it, we have to support him," Justin murmured. "We have to have his back."

What the hell? Did Justin really believe that any good could come out of the challenge? She pressed her lips together and glared over at him. The pain on his face brought her up short. *If he knows what would happen to Brandon, how can he back him?*

"Justin?"

He held up a hand, stopping her. "Talk to Brandon. He knows how I feel already and he needs to know your thoughts, too. But no matter what he decides, we will stand behind him."

Nikki didn't respond, unsure what could be said in the situation. She turned down the gravel road that led to their cabin. It was only a half mile to the house and the entire journey, her mind ran though several possibilities. All of them ended with her losing so much. She pulled up to the front of the house and heard the barking. The sound brought a smile to her lips. Faced with so much new information, it was good to know some things didn't change.

She opened the driver's door without waiting on Justin. She braced her feet shoulder-width apart as the barking came closer. A black streak raced from around her house seconds before a full-blooded sixty-pound black Lab leaped on top of her.

"Hey, Bear." She rubbed the dog from his large front

paws on her shoulders down his back. She received several wet kisses as welcome. God, she'd missed her boy.

Justin's deep laugh came from in front of the house. "Guess he missed you."

She glanced over and her heart swelled. It was obvious the dog wasn't the only one. She wanted Justin to wrap his arms around her and tell her it would be okay. Instead, she let him turn away. This was just as hard on him as her. Except Justin had had to deal with this information much longer. He hadn't had anyone to talk to, with her several miles away. Her job kept her out of the country just as much as it required traveling in the United States. She'd not been there for either man when this had first started. Well, she was home now and Nikki would fix this if she could.

"Justin?" she called before he could make it up the steps.

He turned and raised an eyebrow in question.

"What's the new Alpha's name?"

"Dylan Cross."

She didn't hear him walk into the house—couldn't hear anything over the pounding in her ears. She pushed the dog off her and plopped down on the bottom step.

"*Cross?*" she whispered to the night. Bear lay at her feet and licked her hand. The man she'd met earlier had the last name Cross. Had to be a relation of the new Alpha. She'd picked up on the tension between the two of them outside the café.

Obviously her brother hadn't liked the man. The hostility had been easy enough to read. Because he was related to the new Alpha, or something more? In the normal course of things, she wouldn't have thought anything about getting involved with someone her brother didn't approve of. In fact, that had been how she had picked her high-school boyfriends. But this was something else entirely. Not only was her body almost vibrating at the thought of him, her wolf—who as a rule stayed mostly silent—was scratching and clawing at her to go find him. She could almost taste the strength that had come from the stranger. He might not have been Alpha material, but he had been dominant. And if he was related to the Alpha, that didn't speak well for any challenger.

Brandon had always been quick, strong and smart. However, it scared her to death that it might not be enough this time. He'd never said he'd wanted to lead. In point of fact, the opposite had been true. Brandon had commented several times how he couldn't get paid enough to be Alpha, having no privacy and constant requests to see to. Nikki buried her hands in Bear's thick fur. "What in the world are we going to do?" she asked.

Of course, the dog didn't answer.

The wind picked up, forcing her to return to her Jeep and grab her bag. It smelled like a storm was brewing and she didn't want to get caught out in the rain. Bear stayed with her and she was glad of the company.

She walked in through the front door and the feeling of being home hit her at once. Her eyes blurred from the memories that flooded her. The living room still had the old furniture that had once belonged to her grandparents. The fabric remained worn but clean. The years of spills and rough childhood antics hadn't left too big a mark. The light was off in the dining room and farther back to the kitchen, but she knew no changes had been made there, either. The kitchen would be clean and tidy even if the space needed a new paint job. The table and chairs, old cabinet and expensive wood furnishing in the dining room had been her grandmother's pride and joy. Nikki secretly hoped one day to have those pieces in her house.

The stairs still creaked as she made her way up. She smiled, jumping over the seventh step—the loudest—that had given her away more than once when she'd tried to sneak out as a teen. It was as though that spot had had a direct link to her oldest brother's room.

She passed Brandon's and Justin's rooms on the way to her own. Justin's light shined under his door, but she wanted a little time alone to think things through before she spoke with him again. There had to be something she could do to help Brandon, even if it resulted in her making her brother mad. She would not, could not, accept Brandon challenging for the Alpha position.

Her room hadn't changed a bit in her absence and that was both comforting and sad. Would it really hurt her to visit more than once every couple of years? While she had been traveling and working, her brothers had been trying to figure out the future of the Pack. She did feel terrible that she hadn't wanted to come back. Brandon and Justin had obviously needed her. Bear followed her into the small space and climbed on the bed to plop down.

Hoping a hot shower would clear the exhaustion from travel and help her think more clearly, she dumped her bag onto the bed and grabbed her shower case from it. Nikki had the master bedroom with the bath inside, while Brandon and Justin shared the other bath in the hall. She had told one of them to take her room so they could have the private bath, but Brandon had ignored her and Justin had said as soon as she was mated, he would. She'd answered that in that case it would still be hers for a while.

After turning on the hot water to heat it up, she began to strip. Stepping inside the shower, she sighed and let the steam and heat relax her. The tile in the stall was cracked and stained, but she smiled as she ran her fingertips over the hardness. She'd begged Brandon to decorate her bathroom in pink until at last she'd talked him into it, at about ten years old. He had even found the pink tile for a discount. He'd been that wonderful to her.

It wasn't the décor she'd have picked as an adult, but it had been hers as a child and a teen.

Starting to wash her hair, she thought about the man she had met earlier. RJ was the kind of man she would notice from down the street—his dark good looks, height and build and tattooed arms. She hummed, thinking how damn attractive he'd been. Just the kind of guy she usually found herself attracted to. He'd probably not enjoy showering in the pink space. No, he was more leather and oil. A real man's man.

Yeah, she was sure RJ Cross didn't run around in pink and flowers. She couldn't care less what he preferred. The sexy as sin biker called to the most primal part of her. Nikki craved the dominance male wolves had in them, but in the people she surrounded herself with, she didn't often find what she longed for.

She filled her palms with body wash and ran them down her neck to her chest. Her breasts felt heavy and she wished there was someone in the shower with her. Of course that made her think about RJ again. His large hands would be able to cup her to perfection and his wide, smooth lips would feel fantastic on her skin.

She moved her hands down her body until she skimmed against her mound. She slipped a finger lower, rubbing her clit hard.

Spreading her legs, she leaned on the wall of the shower. The stall would be too small for two people, but she could still imagine RJ on his knees in front of her, licking her folds.

Her imagination and her fingers brought her to the fevered edge she craved. "Oh God," she murmured, sliding two fingers deep inside her pussy. Pumping in and out, she trembled. *Almost right...there...*

A flash of RJ holding her against the wall, his deep voice telling her to come, had her finally falling over the edge.

Spent and warm, she turned off the water and wrapped a towel around her body. She had a lot to think about. Maybe they could come to an understanding, especially if there was interest on both sides. If not, she'd make sure the entire Cross family knew that Brandon had his own support system.

Nikki dressed in a pair of her favorite cotton pants and a tank top prior to unpacking other clothes into her dresser. Nothing seemed to have been moved and the stuff she'd left behind was still inside, but she managed to push it to the back to fit her new additions.

Once everything had been put away, she petted Bear's head then strolled to her window. She pushed aside the white lace curtain to gaze out. Her community was laid out in front of her. The lights from houses that she probably knew every detail of shined in the distance. These people were the only family that she'd ever known. Even if they thought what they were asking Brandon to do was right, Nikki couldn't forgive them for putting her brother in this position.

From a young age, Brandon had taken on the responsibility to make things right around him. If he were being pressured to challenge the Alpha, Nikki couldn't imagine the struggle that he'd been going through.

Maybe she would catch a little nap waiting for Brandon came home. It was time she acted like an adult and showed her brother how much he meant to her. Nikki wasn't going to let him make a decision that might ruin his entire life.

If Brandon could look her in the eye and tell her that he wanted to be Alpha, she would stand behind him. She'd do whatever she needed to keep him safe.

She knew, though, deep in her heart, that Brandon didn't want the job.

It was going to be harder if Brandon admitted he didn't want it.

Either way she'd know for sure what Brandon needed from her.

* * * *

Dylan was already gone by the time RJ made it down the stairs the next morning, but Ben sat dressed in his suit and drinking a cup of coffee.

"'Bout time," his younger brother complained. "I've got to get to work."

RJ frowned as he reached for a clean coffee cup. "So what's stopping you?"

It wasn't as though he usually got up with his brothers.

He liked to work late and had never been an early riser. He enjoyed having his own business so he could set what hours he wanted to work.

"Because I needed to talk to you." Ben stood and rinsed out his coffee mug. RJ moved to the kitchen table his brother had just left and took a seat, waving his hand so Ben would get on with it.

"One of the women I work with said that the Stratton sister would be coming to town," Ben informed him.

RJ froze. He wasn't sure how word of his interaction with the woman would have gotten out already. There had been a lot of people inside the café, but most of them had been from the old Pack.

"From what I understand, she keeps Pack status but hasn't been home in over a year." Ben stared at him.

Striking the most casual pose he could, RJ leaned heavily in his chair. "And?"

"You don't think it's funny that the ceremony and maybe challenge are only days away and she's suddenly back here?"

Now that he thought about it, yes, it was a little strange, but he didn't want to admit it to his brother. He needed to do his own research. "What? You think she's part of the challenge?"

Ben shook his head. "No, of course not, but it doesn't mean they're not up to something."

Ben could be right, but really, what could the young woman do? Besides, she'd flirted with him the previous night. Plus she hadn't even blinked at his name being Cross. He would almost guarantee she hadn't a clue about his family. *Almost* guarantee. He was pretty good at reading people, but he had been distracted by her.

"I'll see what I can find out," he promised. He'd already planned on it, but now he'd do it for his brothers as well. There were favors that RJ could call in if need be. His time in the military had earned him points with several different species, including the Prince of felines.

Ben's shoulders relaxed and guilt turned RJ's stomach. He should tell Ben about having met Nikki Stratton. But instead, he watched his brother pick up his briefcase and waved goodbye. He didn't know why he hesitated. *Fuck, yes, I do.* RJ didn't want Nikki Stratton to be involved in anything against Dylan. *And if she is?* Well, he'd cross that bridge when he got there.

"Where to start?" he asked the empty room. He would treat it like any other investigation as an Enforcer. He picked up his coffee cup, topped it off and made his way to his room and his laptop. He would run some basic searches on Nikki Stratton.

It couldn't be that hard to figure out what the Stratton family and old Pack were up to. Dylan needed to let Cameron know what was going on, whether he wanted to or not. Dylan had told him that he didn't want to worry the Alpha, but Cameron could help in this situation.

He sat down and typed in his password opening the program he'd used when his job had been to do background searches on shifters who had wanted to join the Pack.

When RJ had left, Ben had taken on the task, but RJ still had access to the system.

He typed *Nikki Stratton* into the database and over one hundred results popped up. Okay, he could narrow it down. When he added in *Lawton, New Mexico,* he hit what he was looking for. Nicole Stratton, Lawton Pack, older brothers Brandon and Justin Stratton. Both parents deceased.

RJ sipped as he continued to read.

Fifteen minutes later RJ was impressed with the number of articles written by Nicole B. Stratton. There were so many that he had to print them out to finish reading later. She had traveled to several countries, writing about what she saw and raising awareness of the many cultures that were ignored around the world. It was obvious the woman was good at what she did and that she enjoyed it.

It also raised the question—why would she put that on hold to come home? Why now? And would she be leaving soon?

The last question was purely personal.

The alarm on his watch beeped and he glanced at the time. It was already late morning and he needed to get into town to open his shop, even if the people who came only wanted to check out the new Alpha's brother. He might not be giving out tattoos, but he'd get good intel. The Pack members who had moved to Lawton with them stopped by to share what they were hearing, while the original residents wanted to see him up close and personal.

He stuffed the articles into his top desk drawer after logging off his computer. Until he decided what to do about Nikki, he didn't want either of his brothers to know what he was doing. Yes, he'd told Ben, but he also needed time to sort through how much to tell Dylan. Ben never could keep a secret, so RJ would have to let him remain in the dark as well.

He showered quickly before dressing in a faded pair of jeans and a black T-shirt. His custom boots and jacket followed. After locking up behind himself, he peered out into the dreary weather. The thunderstorms from the previous night had quieted down to a steady light fall of rain. He could still ride his bike, but he didn't like feeling damp denim against his body for the rest of the day.

Instead of heading to where he'd parked his bike under the carport, RJ followed the deck around to the large garage that hid behind the house. He rarely drove a car, but when he did it was going to be the type that he wanted. Southeast New Mexico might not be the place for a classic, but RJ didn't care. He'd wanted to own a sixty-seven Impala his entire life. Now, with money in the bank from his years of service, he could take his time restoring the beauty.

His baby wasn't perfect yet, but she would be. Since no one was setting up appointments for tattoos, maybe RJ would try to divide his time better and schedule working on his ride.

It would be fun to pull her out today, though.

The bay doors squeaked as RJ opened them. The storage garage was old but clean and tidy. Of course, since Dylan also stored a vehicle back here, it had to be. His older brother wouldn't stand for a dirty area, even to work on cars.

RJ shook his head. He had no idea how Dylan could be so fussy but love to get dirty at as well.

As he pulled the cover from his car, he admired the sleek lines and ran his hand over the body. When he'd seen this particular model had been on a television show and he'd been drooling over it ever since. The only one he'd been able to find had been a beaten-down black model in the rear of someone's yard. RJ had purchased it and sent the car on to Dylan to house until RJ returned.

The hours he and the members of his unit had spent tearing out old fabric, rebuilding the engine and adding personal touches stayed with him. When he looked at his car, he could remember the good times they'd had fixing her up. The beer had been cold, the laughter plentiful and his best friends by his side. That was before Casey had found his mate and the missions had started to weigh on them all.

Back in a simpler time that RJ needed to hold on to.

Plus, the Impala was a chick magnet. He wondered what Nikki had planned that morning. If she hadn't known who he was the previous night, surely she did by now. It might make it more difficult to get closer to her, but he'd always been a determined man. RJ wouldn't trade on his attraction to her to get information on her brother, but a woman with the integrity to write the articles he'd read couldn't be behind a hostile takeover. He counted on it.

There might even be a chance that he'd win her over to his side, keeping a challenge from occurring. Because he had right on his side.

Cameron had chosen his brother to lead the Pack. It angered him that the old Alpha's wishes were not being respected, in addition to the fact that he wouldn't stand for any threat against his family.

The rumble of the Impala was loud in the quietness of the garage. He reversed out, speed slow, and headed toward town. Brandon Stratton had already pulled him over once. It had been a tense battle of strength between the two men. RJ knew the sheriff had been testing his control, pushing RJ's buttons to see what he would do. RJ had managed to hang on to his wolf and not give the sheriff what he wanted. After taking the speeding ticket, he thought he'd seen a flash of respect in Brandon's eyes, but he couldn't be sure.

He took the side streets until he reached the alley in which he parked. The drive had been way too short, but after work, he'd take her toward the flatlands where he could really open the old girl up and not worry about getting a ticket.

RJ entered his shop through the back door and flipped on the lights. The place remained neat and clean from the prior night. Everything was in place. Of course, the top-grade security system he'd had installed would have warned him if anything had been wrong, but being cautious was ingrained in RJ. His footsteps echoed as he crossed the front entry to the windows and doors. He opened the blinds, letting the bright sunlight in to gleam off the stainless steel countertops. He reached for the Open sign when he spotted several older residents standing across the street, looking in his direction.

"Let's see what this is about," he murmured. RJ did turn the sign around before unlocking the front door and stepping outside. For an instant, he regretted not wearing his sunglasses. The day hadn't called for the dark shades, but he enjoyed the ability to intimidate people. The few old men who were hanging out across the street hadn't been welcoming to RJ or his family at all.

In front of his glass window RJ leaned back and crossed his arms over his chest. He stared at the group and, just as he suspected, they began to look everywhere but at him.

He'd seen the tall, gray-haired man, Todd Stewart, talking with Brandon Stratton several times in the past two weeks.

RJ's instincts were telling him that Todd was the main voice trying to get the challenge against Dylan started. Todd wouldn't be able to win versus RJ's brother, so he needed someone who might.

As dominant and strong as Brandon Stratton was, RJ didn't believe that he'd take out Dylan in a fair fight. Which meant that something more sinister was in the works. It didn't take more than five minutes of RJ's presence on the sidewalk to have the small group strolling away.

Half a block down, Todd turned toward RJ.

RJ dipped his head. He'd promised not to start trouble, but he also wouldn't allow anyone to intimidate him. Todd sneered then retreated.

"RJ!"

He spun around, not having heard anyone coming up behind him. The pretty young woman on the sidewalk grinned at him.

"Are you causing trouble?" she asked.

"No, ma'am," he replied on autopilot. Trisha and RJ had grown up together and had been good friends through high school. During his absence, she'd mated a quiet but friendly shifter she'd met during college. RJ hadn't been surprised when Dylan had told him she'd offered to move Packs with him. Trisha's mate, Eli, was from around these parts. If RJ remembered correctly, Eli's old Pack lived about an hour or so away.

Forgetting all about the old men, RJ smiled down at the petite woman. "You look good," he said. "How're things going?"

"Great!" She bounced a little as she spoke. "Eli is meeting me at the coffee café, but I wanted to stroll around the shops first. I can't believe Dylan and Ben managed to get everything going so fast. I thought it would take much longer to get set up."

So had he. "Ben said that over the years, several stores and services here had gone out of business. Economic downturn and all that." He waved his hand. RJ didn't understand half of what Ben had tried to explain to him. As a real estate manager, Ben kept his finger in a lot of pies and always knew what went on with companies. "What have you been up to?"

"Oh." Trisha beamed. "I got hired on to teach history at the high school. With the addition of our Pack, the town needs more help at the schools. They had most of the young pups in a building and grouped them together per grades. Now there's enough for us to have full classes. The teachers at the schools are really excited."

"That's great!" RJ really needed to hear about some good things happening.

"One of the teachers from here is even organizing meetings with the school district for upgrading the facilities. He seems to have a lot of support already, so I hope it'll go through. I offered to help him," Trisha said.

"Wow." RJ wanted to hug his old friend. While he'd been so busy worrying about the upcoming Alpha switch, someone in the community had stepped up for the children. "Who's this guy? Maybe I could offer some help once he gets approval for the improvements."

"His name is Justin Stratton," Trisha said.

"Stratton?" *Can I not get away from that damn family?*

"You probably know his brother." Trisha sounded excited. "He's the sheriff."

Oh, RJ knew the sheriff all right. He couldn't tell Trisha that, though. "Yeah. I'll see if I can get hold of Justin and find out what he might need."

"Awesome!" Trisha grabbed his arm. "This has been such a good move for us."

"I'm glad," RJ responded.

"Well, I'd better finish my window shopping. I don't want to be late for coffee with my mate."

RJ gave her a little wave as she skipped off. At least she was happy. He didn't know how she could appear so oblivious to the tensions in the town. He watched as she stopped to talk to someone else. The women, an original resident, seemed friendly, though. They exchanged a few words before Trisha took off again. Maybe the Pack would fare better than his own family. That boded well if a challenge didn't take place.

RJ spun to return into his shop. He had a long day of staring at his sketch book. If he didn't get any real customers soon, he'd go crazy. Money wasn't an issue, but RJ was used to being busy. He needed to keep his hands and mind occupied.

One thing he knew — he shouldn't be thinking about the Stratton siblings.

His first priority was to his brother. Being an Alpha should be the perfect opportunity for Dylan and it was RJ's job to protect him. He'd been gone and left his brothers on their own for too long.

Not that RJ didn't love what he'd done. The training had been superior and the friends he'd made were an addition to his family. But going back to civilian life wasn't an easy transition.

"I just need to draw," he mumbled to himself. RJ could always use another tattoo. Once he completed the art work, he'd call Mike or Casey to come ink him.

Chapter Three

Nikki had slept like the dead. She'd meant to be awake when Brandon had gotten off shift, but she hadn't heard a thing once she'd passed out in bed. Upon waking, she had been thrown for a minute unable to place where she'd fallen asleep. Then the memory of the trouble they could be in had had her stomach in knots as she had dressed for the day.

She looked forward to seeing her friend again, but she now wished she hadn't invited her to breakfast. She needed to have a conversation with her brother. Nikki moved quietly around the house, starting the coffeepot and turning on the television. She needed to fix breakfast.

The familiar routine helped to settle her. Growing up, she'd had to learn to cook since both Brandon and Justin had proved to be disasters in the kitchen. She placed the cinnamon rolls in the oven when Brandon appeared in the doorway. Nikki poured him a cup and set it on the bar between them.

He grunted his thanks and took a seat. Brandon appeared tired, more worn-out than she'd seen the previous night. If she'd been paying better attention when she'd arrived, Nikki might have realized sooner that something was wrong. She placed the spatula she held on the counter then leaned against the bar.

Brandon drank half the coffee before he glanced up at her. "Justin told you?"

Nikki nodded. *Guess we're were going to do this now.* "How could you even consider it?" she asked, her voice soft.

He peered down, rubbing the side of his mug. "I hadn't,

really. Some of the older members approached me and I figured they were just upset and would get over it."

"But they didn't," she guessed.

"No. As the ceremony gets closer, they're getting more desperate. Word is that Dylan Cross will fill his inner circle with his own wolves. Cameron's discussed that some of our Pack would be involved, but I guess Dylan is backing out on that. So we would be losing the Pack and that scares people. Especially if the shifters do go public soon, as planned. If I don't do it, then someone else will."

"Someone not as strong as you," she filled in. Nikki couldn't even imagine the pressure Brandon was under. He didn't answer, so she just watched him, the man who had been her mother and father for the last twenty years. "Do you even want to be Alpha?" she asked when he remained silent.

He glanced up and she read the answer in his eyes. He didn't, but he felt trapped.

She walked around the counter and wrapped an arm around his neck. "I don't want to lose you," she whispered into his ear.

He hugged her tight and they just held each other. Nikki couldn't believe this was happening. She had to find a way to save them all. "We'll figure it out," she promised.

Brandon gave her one last squeeze before letting her go and standing. "In two days? I've been trying to come up with another way for months now. And I don't want you to get involved. I just wanted you home. I wanted to have some time with you."

Nikki bit her lip at the lost look on his face. She had never understood how much responsibility her brother carried. "I love you."

He smiled, just the corners of his lips curving up. "I love you, too."

"But I'm not staying out of anything."

Brandon sighed. "We don't know what's going to happen."

"I know what's *not* going to happen. I'm not losing my brother!"

"Nik—"

"No." She shook her head. "I've been thinking about this. You didn't have to support me when I wanted to go away for school. Hell, you paid for college. If it wasn't for you, I don't know where I'd have ended up."

"You were meant for great things. You'd have found your own way."

Jesus, does it take something like Brandon's possible death for us to talk like this? "I can't live without you."

"No!" He grabbed her face. "If something happens to me, you and Justin need to get out of here. Take him to Houston with you."

"This is our home," she argued.

"If I have to challenge, it won't be any longer."

"How'd we get here?" she asked. "Why is this happening?"

"I don't know. I still have two days. Maybe I'll think of something."

"Just don't do it," she practically begged him.

"I gotta get ready for work. Just yell when breakfast is ready."

She watched him go, her chest aching. Nikki loved her family. If something happened to Brandon and she'd wasted so much time staying away, she'd never be able to make that up to him. Her brother was the greatest man she knew. No—Nikki wouldn't let this happen. She needed to come up with a plan. Shit, she wrote pieces that had an entire world stepping up to help others. When it really mattered, Nikki would use everything at her disposal.

Her travels had taken her all over and she'd made friends with numerous shifters of different species. If it came down to calling in favors, she'd do it. Nikki didn't have long to think about it. The back door opened and the whirlwind of her best friend entered. Hands full of bags and children, Sabrina swept in, distracting her from her problems.

Breakfast was a noisy but wonderful event. The kids

woke Justin up, so he made it down right behind Brandon. They shared a look of worry but both remained quiet. After a while, both men went off to work, leaving the women and kids. Sabrina ushered the two older kids into the den to watch television as Nikki sat with another cup of coffee at the table, holding baby Julian.

Sabrina topped off the mugs before sitting beside her.

"How are things around here?" her friend asked.

Nikki was glad she'd brought it up. She didn't want to confide too much, but she needed to talk to someone. "As well as can be expected."

Sabrina sent her a sympathetic look. "I know a lot of the other members of the Pack are worried, but I don't know that a challenge is the way to go. Cameron is giving his blessing for the new Alpha. He's been working on the transition being as smooth as possible. I think it's a great idea of Dylan's to bring the Pack members in prior to taking over, so everyone could merge together."

Nikki was glad her friend agreed. "How's it been around here since the new members came? Any problems?"

"No, as far as I've heard, they've brought in more money, businesses and are a pretty good bunch."

"Then why all this talk about the challenge?"

Sabrina shrugged. "It's mostly the older generation. You know how they are about change. And this is a big one."

"Yeah, but Cameron wouldn't bring someone in he didn't trust. It couldn't have been easy to decide. He even consulted the Alpha council."

"I know. So much has happened within the shifter world in the last few months. Talking about going public, the feline Prince being kidnapped and now a new leader here. They're just trying to control something."

Nikki thought about the new information. "Does Cameron know? He should be able to do something."

"I don't think so. He wouldn't want a challenge. He would for sure try to talk to Brandon. But what can you say? I haven't actually heard if Brandon is going to challenge. Just the rumor that he should."

"Someone has to tell Cameron," Nikki insisted.

"And if Brandon doesn't challenge, it could put him in jeopardy. What would you do in his position? He can't act on a rumor."

"What do you know about the new Alpha?"

"Just that he was an Enforcer at his old Pack. He showed all the signs of being a great leader, but their Pack had several wolves descended from the Alpha who would want the position. To be an Alpha, he had to go somewhere else."

She had to ask, Nikki knew, but she dreaded bringing up the name. "What do you know about his brother, RJ Cross?"

Sabrina grinned. "Good-looking, smart, but a little rough around the edges. He owns the tattoo parlor in town, drives a Harley and has every woman in town lusting after him."

"Hmm," Nikki murmured, not one hundred percent happy that the thought of every woman in town making eyes at the stranger made her feel extremely jealous. *Damn, I've just met the guy.*

"He has another brother, too," Sabrina informed her.

"Really?"

"Younger than Dylan and RJ. He works at the real estate office with Max. Max says he's quiet and keeps to himself. Nice and wicked smart."

"So both the brothers already work in town?" That was good information. If she wanted to protect her brother, she needed as much intel as she could find on them.

"Yep, why? What are you going to do?" Sabrina asked with a nervous laugh.

"I don't know yet."

"Well, whatever you do, it has to be quick." Sabrina stood. Nikki passed the baby over to her. "Not everyone wants a challenge, but if there is one, sides will be drawn. Brandon would have the entire town on his. That's a lot of pressure."

Picking up the mugs and a few plates from the kitchen, Nikki couldn't help but agree. If she was going to help, she needed to get started. First, she needed to find out more about the entire Cross family.

As soon as Sabrina had gone, Nikki fetched her laptop from her room. She took it over to the kitchen counter. She refreshed her coffee then settled in. She knew she had better programs than some of the law enforcement agencies. The different papers that published her work relied on an honest take and detailed articles from her. She paid good money to be able to access people's personal information. Normally, she hated having to stoop to use the databases, but this time Nikki felt no guilt. If invading the Cross brothers' privacy would save her brother, then Nikki had work to do.

As much as she wanted to start with RJ, she typed in Dylan's name first. It was the responsible decision to make. Plus, if she learned enough about Dylan to put her mind at ease, maybe she wouldn't even have to research RJ. Nikki would much prefer to learn about him first-hand. But if she had doubts, Nikki would find out everything she could about the man, from what he liked for breakfast to his color of underwear. Hopefully he wasn't a boxers kind of guy. Nikki enjoyed a well-defined package.

* * * *

RJ lifted his head from his new art work at the sound of a door slamming close by. Nikki Stratton stood, hands on hips, glaring at the front entrance of his shop. He grinned; closing his sketchpad then slipped it under the counter. Since the last three pictures had been of her in different sexual positions, it sure wouldn't be wise for her to see it.

He adjusted his hard cock as she stomped toward his door with long, confident strides. Nikki had dressed in an almost identical style to his. Faded jeans and a snug, fitted black T-shirt with black sneakers. Her long hair was pulled up into a ponytail and he could almost imagine hanging on to her hair as she went down on him. He licked his lips in need. *Probably wasn't smart to have been fantasizing about her for the past hour.*

Damn, she looks determined.

Everything he had learned from the Internet made him think she would attack any problem head-on. Hopefully he could get her on his side. Not against her brother, but against a challenge.

She pushed open the door, only pausing a second to take in the lack of customers before turning and moving the sign to Closed. He allowed her to walk around the shop, taking in his pride and joy without interruption. While she prowled, he admired her. After several moments, she peered over at him.

"We have a problem," she said.

"Just one?" he asked, crossing his arms. He could think of at least half a dozen issues. Of course, he knew exactly what she was talking about.

She laughed. "One problem at a time, I think."

"Okay." He waved to one of the couches. "Have a seat."

Nikki sat and he chose one of the other chairs so he could be directly in front of her. He wanted to sit close, but he wasn't sure if he did that he would be able to keep his hands off her. It'd be better that he put some distance between them—for now, anyway. She smelled clean and fresh. He closed his eyes for a second and took a deep breath, pulling her scent inside him. When he opened his eyes again, she was sitting staring down at her hands.

"Which problem would you like to discuss today?" he asked. He didn't like the thought of her being upset. The urge to join her on the couch was strong once again. Shit, she should be considered the enemy, but instead he felt a need inside him that was new. If the guys in his unit could see him pining for some chick he didn't know, they'd have a good laugh at him.

"Our brothers."

RJ tensed. He didn't mean to, but he couldn't hide his reaction. As soon as he did, she shifted away from him. He took several deep breaths in the hopes of calming himself and putting her at ease.

"I have heard rumors," he admitted, not wanting to give too much away until he knew her stance. "It concerns me."

"It *concerns* you? That's all you have to say? Just an everyday nuisance? Don't you want to do something to stop it?"

RJ laughed. *This spitfire of a woman is sure intriguing.* "You've been here, what? Twelve hours? I've been here for weeks. In all that time, not one person has asked my opinion. And if they did, I would tell them that Cameron chose his replacement and the members of this community need to accept it."

She frowned and shook her head. "What's your brother going to do about it?"

"What's my brother going to do? Are you saying Brandon is going to challenge?"

"No!" It came out almost as a yell. She caught herself and cleared her throat. "No, I'm not saying that. But there are people in this town who don't want your brother to be Alpha. He needs to address it."

Even though the entire situation was serious, he admired the woman sitting across from him. But she did have some fucking nerve coming in and making demands of his family. They were on the right side of things. "My brother plans on accepting the position of the Alpha of the Lawton Pack as requested by the current Alpha Cameron King," he told her, his tone formal. "He does not have to prove his worth to anyone and does not have to ask permission. This has already been decided."

She snorted. "Nice. Nicely worded."

He liked that she appreciated it. It had never been his job to be diplomatic. That was Ben's specialty.

"And you know that's a bullshit answer. I didn't expect that from you. Maybe from Ben, but I thought you would shoot a little straighter."

RJ tensed and a growl slipped out. "What do you know about Ben?"

"Not much. Doesn't seem like anyone knows much

more than that he keeps to himself and he's very smart. A good businessman who's invested in the growth of our community."

Her words filled him with pride. Ben was smart, even though that caused him to keep to himself so much. Being bullied as a kid would do that to a guy. Dylan and RJ had done their best to protect him, but they hadn't always succeeded.

"Dylan hasn't been around much, either. Spending all his time with Cameron," she commented.

"He does have a new Pack to learn about," RJ replied.

"Then there's you. You placed yourself right smack in the middle of town, you mix with the community and you stay visible. Like you're trying to take everyone's attention from your brothers. Does that sound about right?"

She was smart. But so was he. "And you. The big-city girl comes home, asks about the Cross brothers and thinks she knows it all?" he questioned.

"No, I don't know it all. But I do know that in two days, one way or another, we will have a new Alpha. If there is a challenge of any form, it will tear this town apart. You might not care about that, but this is my family we're talking about, my town."

"Maybe you should be talking to the people in *your* town who are causing problems."

"I plan to," she said. "But first I want to know what your brother is planning."

"I just told you," RJ stated firmly. "If you want to know something else, you'll have to ask him."

"If he is challenged, will he fight?" she asked.

"I can't answer that."

Nikki pressed her lips together before sucking her bottom lip, most likely in thought. His cock responded right away, growing harder as he stared at her mouth. Damn it—they were having a serious conversation and he still wanted to mount her. Just the thought that she was brave enough to ask questions no one else had made him want to strip her naked and pound into her. She licked her lips and he stifled a moan.

The fantasy from the previous night returned. Her on her knees in front of him, pleasing him with her mouth and hands. His cock started leaking against the front of his jeans and he shifted, trying to relieve some of the pressure.

Her cough brought his thoughts back to the current time. When he glanced over at her, she stared at his lap. His erection was obvious under the zipper of his pants.

"Really?" she asked, peeking up at him.

He grinned and winked. "What can I say?" RJ wouldn't defend his body's reaction. She had to know how attractive she was. Hell, she might be attempting to play him for more information.

She chewed on her lip more and he groaned. Her eyebrows drew together in her confusion.

"Stop with the lip thing! You're killing me here."

Her eyes widened. "Hmm," she teased and darted her tongue to swipe at her lips.

He wasn't a saint. His control could only be tested so far. He jumped off the chair and was on her in one second. He straddled her legs and pushed her against the couch.

"You're playing with fire, Nikki Stratton," he warned. Any indication she wanted this to go forward and he would be all over her. RJ jerked while she ran her hands up from his knees to his waist.

"Oh, God, just kiss me," she pleaded, tilting her head back.

"Hell yeah." He celebrated for a quick second before leaning down and closing the distance between their mouths, nice and slow.

Sweet and tender wasn't his normal speed but RJ felt he needed to take his time. He licked at the seam of her lips forcing his tongue through. She opened for him and their tongues met, her hands gripped his shoulders hard as well.

He made love to her mouth like he planned to soon do to her body.

Eventually the need to breathe forced him to draw away. He almost laughed when she licked her lips, which had started the entire thing.

"We can't do this," she whispered.

RJ nodded. He was disappointed, but she was right. Instead of giving in and getting another taste of her, RJ climbed off her and strode across the room to the small fridge he had under the counter. As he pulled out two waters, he took deep breaths, trying to regain his control. He had a feeling that Nikki would be doing the same thing behind him. Once he knew he wouldn't pounce on the woman, he spun away.

He passed her a bottle before sitting back down.

"Thanks." Her voice still sounded strained. RJ hid his smile by taking a drink.

"Should I apologize?" Their present situation made what had happened highly inappropriate, but they'd both wanted it.

Nikki snorted. "We're both adults. I think we can own up to a kiss and agree that we have more important things to deal with."

So we're back to our brothers.

"Got any ideas?" she asked.

Oh, RJ had several, but since they all ended with her on her back, he decided not to voice them.

"Come on," she exclaimed. "We have two days to figure something out."

"Answer this," RJ demanded. "Does Brandon want to be Alpha?"

For several moments he didn't think she'd answer, but at last she shook her head.

He raised his bottle and tilted it to her. "You need to convince your brother not to challenge Dylan."

"Yeah, why didn't I think of that?" Nikki rolled her eyes. "It's not that simple and you know it."

He disagreed. "But it is. Dylan was picked by Cameron King. The Pack needs to respect his wishes."

"The Pack is worried. They don't know your brother, your family or anyone else. They have the right to be concerned," she shot back.

"If they believe in Cameron, why are they questioning his choice? I've met the man several times and I don't see him turning his Pack over to someone who will lead them down the wrong road. Do you even know why they don't accept Dylan?"

"Not exactly."

"That's bullshit, then. He's a good man and he'll be a great and fair leader."

"He's new and different."

He snorted and took a long drink. "So instead of using these last two weeks or even the few months we've been here getting to know the future Alpha or asking questions, they come up with a conspiracy to get rid of him."

"It's not a conspiracy," she argued.

"They had their time to talk with Cameron. To ask questions. Instead they wait until days prior to the ceremony then they start speaking about a challenge?"

"If Brandon doesn't challenge, then someone else will."

With a jerk of his shoulder, RJ sat forward. "Fine, then they should expect a fight."

"It's nothing against you or your family."

"Yes, actually it is. Dylan is meant to be the Alpha. But dividing the Pack was never meant to happen. Even if Dylan wins the challenge, he'll constantly be reminded he's not from here. How is that fair?"

"He had to know, coming here, something like this might happen."

"No," he interrupted. "We were told we were wanted here. That it had already been decided. Dylan doesn't deserve this."

"What about his inner circle? Is he only using the wolves he brought with him?"

RJ shook his head. "I don't know. I do know that Cameron and Dylan have discussed it, but that is something that we'd have to ask him. Why?"

"Just some rumors that Dylan is using this to bring his Pack up and leave the original Pack in the dust."

"Dylan wouldn't do that!"

Nikki slammed her water on the side table while she sank against the couch. "This isn't going to work. If we can't agree, then we'll never get the Pack to."

"I don't know."

"I think the majority of the Pack, both new and old members, are okay with it," she said. "Just a handful of the people, really, have any concerns. They just need to hash all this out and it doesn't look like there's much communication."

"That's a good idea. Maybe they should just get together and have it out before the ceremony."

"Unless they kill each other."

"I think they can both resist the urge. Plus we'll be there to help keep things calm. Bring Justin as well."

"We need to do it soon and without anyone else knowing about it. Can you get Brandon to our house tonight?" he requested.

She hesitated then nodded. "Yeah, if I don't tell him where we're going, I think I might manage it. He doesn't get off work until ten, though."

"Midnight?" he offered. RJ didn't know how he'd get both of his brothers to stay up that late without explaining what was going on. But it was worth a shot.

"Okay," she agreed, standing.

"Kiss for the road?" he teased. He couldn't resist.

She flipped him off, obviously trying not to smile.

"Fine. Be that way." RJ rose. Whatever was happening between them was far from over.

"I'll see you tonight," she said. "Hopefully."

"Wait," he called out, stopping her progress. "We should exchange numbers."

"Should we?" she asked.

"For our brothers," he quipped.

This time Nikki laughed and the sound was magical. She pulled her cell from her pocket. "What's your number?"

"You naughty girl," RJ said. "I knew you liked me. First you ask for my number then you'll be stalking me for a date."

"Wow!" she said. "Does that act ever work?"

RJ gave her his best fake pout. "Act?"

She waved her phone. "Just tell me."

He gave in and got her digits in return. He *did* want it for the reasons he'd said, but he could already picture all the dirty texts he could send her. What did kids call it these days? *Sexting.* Yeah, he wanted to sext her.

"I'll call if I have any problems getting Brandon to agree," she told him.

"Be careful," he said then peered out of the front window. "There's a good chance that you were either spotted coming in or someone has seen your vehicle."

"Don't worry about me," she dismissed. "Just start thinking about what we're going to say tonight."

She'd gone not allowing him to formulate a reply. *What an interesting turn of events.* He'd somehow managed to secure support from at least one Stratton, plus he had a better idea of what was going on. If Brandon truly didn't want the position of Alpha, he'd be a fool to challenge Dylan. Now they just needed to figure out how to get Dylan and Brandon on the same side.

Chapter Four

Fresh from the shower, nervous and almost desperate, Nikki drove down the empty roads with Brandon beside her and Justin in the back seat. She'd expected more questions, but the men must have seen something in her face that convinced them, so that when she'd said they needed to come with her, they had.

She tried tell them something, but every time she opened her mouth, she couldn't get the words out.

"Nik," Brandon called softly. "What's going on?"

She had to give him credit that he had remained quiet for so long. In only a few more minutes, they would pull up to the house RJ and his brothers shared. "I need you to trust me, Brandon. To know that I love you more than anything."

"I do trust you," he assured her.

"Then you have to do what is right."

"What are you talking about?" He covered her hand on the wheel. She released her grip and held on to him. "You're scaring me," he said, kissing her hand.

"Brandon, please trust me." She made the turn to the Cross house, feeling him tense next to her.

"What did you do? Nikki, why are we here?"

She shook her head and continued to drive.

"Stop the car," he ordered.

It took all her willpower to remove her hand from his hold and put it back on the wheel to continue toward the house.

"Nicole Stratton, pull this car over!"

She whimpered at the tone, her wolf wanting her to obey the dominant wolf next to her. It wasn't often that he used the big guns. But Nikki had to remain strong. This was for his own good. "Please, Brandon." She pressed her foot down on the gas pedal, moving them quicker not wanting to lose her nerve. The house came into sight, with RJ standing on the porch.

She drove up in front of him and took a deep breath. "Just come inside. Talk to Dylan, work this out. I beg you."

Brandon growled long and low. Nikki shuddered. He was pissed. The scent of fury that filled the car actually made her nauseous.

"Oh, shit!" Justin barked a laugh from the back seat. "This is actually a good idea."

Brandon snarled at him and wrapped his hand around Nikki's upper arm. "What were you thinking?"

She shook, his anger hard for her to handle, but she had to try.

"Get us out of here," he demanded, shaking her a little. He was still in control, making sure he didn't hurt her, but she still wanted to roll over for him.

"Too late," Justin piped up. "Look."

They glanced toward the porch, where two other men had joined RJ.

"Just talk to him," she begged her brother.

"Come on, man." Justin gripped Brandon's shoulder. "What have you got to lose? I can't believe that no one else thought of this sooner. And I thought I was the smart one in the family."

"You're not funny," Brandon told him.

"I'm not trying to be," Justin replied. "It's either this or you challenge him and possibly die. You might be okay with that but Nik and I aren't. We need our big brother."

"We'll discuss this later," Brandon warned her.

Oh, I have no doubt.

Brandon leaped away, throwing his door open then slamming it closed. Nikki and Justin scrambled to catch up. They met at the front of her Jeep. Nikki peered over the two men she hadn't met, but her eyes were drawn to RJ. His gaze flickered to her but settled on Brandon, his body full of tension. No one moved for several moments.

"This isn't a good idea," Brandon whispered to her.

"It's all I could come up with," she said. "The ceremony is in two days."

"Less than," Justin added.

"When this all goes to shit I want the two of you to get out of here," Brandon ordered. "Do not worry about me. You are not to get hurt."

Jesus, does Brandon expect to be attacked? She glanced toward RJ. *Has he set me up?* "We're not leaving you."

"Promise!" Brandon demanded in a low tone.

"Yes," she managed. Nikki did not feel good about her decision to trick Brandon into meeting with Dylan. *What if he gets hurt?* All this had the potential to blow up in her face.

"Justin?" Brandon pressed.

"Okay," Justin agreed. Nikki didn't think that Justin would leave Brandon alone any more than she planned to. This was one promise that she'd have no problem with breaking.

Brandon straightened his shoulders. He looked like a man about to face a firing squad.

Nikki had fucked up. If RJ betrayed her, she'd find a means to get him back. He'd suffer in the worst way possible if she had any say about things. As much as she wanted to trust RJ, she had some serious doubts. His comment from earlier that she'd strolled into town thinking she could solve this problem bothered her. Brandon must have his reasons for not going to Cameron or the new Alpha. Yep, Nikki had once again gotten caught up in trying to save the world without thinking things through. If they made it out of this meeting unharmed, she owed her oldest brother an apology.

Or maybe she was brilliant.

"Let's do this," she muttered, opening the door. Hiding her concerns from both her family and the Cross brothers she could do. Besides, she didn't in fact know this would backfire.

All Nikki needed to do was have faith. *Forget the moments of reservations. This needs to work.*

RJ watched as the three Stratton siblings stood together, Nikki placed between the two brothers just like he and Dylan had put Ben. No one moved or spoke. He'd convinced Ben to help set Dylan up to meet with Brandon, but now, with the tension flowing through all the shifters, he had to wonder if it had been a good idea. Nikki's distress was evident in her face and it took all his control not to go down and comfort her.

Ben broke the silence. "Please, won't you all come inside so we can talk?"

Brandon glanced at his siblings before he nodded and started toward the house. RJ never took his eyes from the pissed-off shifter, though. Dylan, for his part, seemed loose and relaxed, but RJ could tell he was just as wary. Ben turned and led the way inside. Brandon, Nikki and Justin followed with RJ after and Dylan bringing up the rear.

The biggest room was the den and that was where they headed.

"Please sit and be comfortable," Ben invited.

Brandon took one of the recliners and Nikki sat on the couch while Justin shifted nervously from foot to foot.

"I just put some coffee on. Let me bring it in," Ben stated once everyone was in the room.

"I'll help you," Justin offered.

Dylan took the recliner across from Brandon. RJ squeezed his shoulder when he passed and sat on the fireplace hearth across the room. He hoped by taking himself out of the situation, Dylan and Brandon could work something out. The emotions in the room were almost stifling and he didn't need another display of aggression between his brother and the sheriff.

"Thank you for coming," Dylan began until Brandon snorted.

"Like I had much of a choice?" Brandon accused.

Nikki pressed her hands together in her lap, seeming guilty.

Dylan sighed and leaned forward. "It seems to me my brother and your sister had a little more sense than us. We should have met earlier."

Some of the fury seemed to leave Brandon after he took deep breaths. Brandon glanced at his sister and RJ watched them lock gazes. Brandon's eyes narrowed. It was clear when Brandon realized something more was going on.

"You son of a bitch!" Brandon yelled and launched himself at RJ.

RJ took a hard knock as Brandon's fist hit his chin. His head snapped back and he tasted blood in his mouth. He vaguely heard Nikki scream and Dylan hollered. He managed to block the next punch to his head but missed the left to his stomach. Dylan pulled Brandon from him and pushed him across the room to face off against him. From the corner of his eye, he saw Ben and Justin rush into the room.

"Brandon, stop!" Nikki tried to grab her brother, but he pushed her behind him.

RJ growled, but Dylan blocked his path. "No, we finish this now. If you have a problem with my family, you come through me," Dylan told Brandon.

"Is this going to be how you run the Pack?" Brandon spat at him. "You have a problem and you send in one of your brothers to seduce an innocent?"

"No!" Nikki gasped.

Dylan had obviously been caught off-guard, because he took a step away and faced him. "RJ?"

RJ laughed. "Are you serious?" he asked Brandon. "Have you met your sister? She's the last person who'd allow anyone to get one over on her."

"Because you know her so well?" Brandon pressed.

"Better than you, obviously," RJ responded.

"Not helping," Dylan warned him.

He couldn't believe this. RJ had taken a chance trying to

get this asshole in the same room with his brother and the guy accused him of using Nikki for his own gain. "Come on, Dy, you know me. This is bullshit."

Dylan stared at him as he searched RJ's face for something. At last, he nodded. Dylan turned to Brandon. "I do know my brother. And whatever you think, you have it wrong. But this isn't about them. It's about us. Do you want to challenge me? You want to do this now?"

Brandon still fumed. "Fuck you. This is about all of us. If I didn't want to challenge you before, you crossed a line tonight. She" — he pointed at his sister — "has nothing to do with this."

"Brandon—" Nikki started.

"No, I don't want to be the damn Alpha. I never did. But I won't let this Pack belong to someone with such little consideration and respect. This is just too much. Do you know what is going to happen in three months when we go public? No, none of us do. We have to trust our leader."

Brandon grabbed Nikki's arm and pulled her toward the door.

"Wait!" Nikki dug her heels in. "Just listen to me."

"We'll talk about this in the car or at home. We're leaving now." He tugged her again.

"We'll talk about this now," Nikki argued and yanked her arm from his hold. "RJ didn't seduce me or whatever you think happened."

"Nik, this isn't the time or place."

"We didn't do anything wrong and certainly not what you're thinking. I thought you knew me better than that."

The hurt in her voice had RJ wanting to punch Brandon. He massaged his jaw where Brandon's fist had landed. If Brandon fucked this up, RJ wouldn't take it easy on him. So they'd kissed. That didn't have anything to do with trying to fix the issue of him challenging the incoming Alpha. "Dylan and Ben didn't even know we were coming up with this. Can we please just sit down and try this again?"

"Brandon…" Justin moved from the doorway to his

brother. "We need to hear Nikki out."

Brandon looked torn, but eventually he nodded. Ben gripped Dylan's shoulder and led him back to the chair. Once Brandon and Dylan were settled in their seats and Ben and Justin on the couch, Nikki stayed standing by her oldest brother. RJ wanted to reassure her, pull her into his arms, do something to help. But he stood silent while she worked out what she wanted to say.

"First, let me clear up one thing. I went to RJ," Nikki informed them. "I'm sorry, Brandon, but I couldn't let the Pack pressure you into doing something you didn't want. I understand you have to look out for the Pack. But you're my brother and I have to look out for you."

Brandon opened his mouth but straight away snapped it shut. Instead of speaking, he just nodded.

"I knew you didn't actually want to be Alpha. I also know that Dylan doesn't want to meet you in a challenge. A challenge would leave one of us" — she gestured between her and RJ — "without one of the people we love the most."

"Why him?" Brandon questioned.

"That's a little more difficult to explain." She glanced around the room.

Oh, this is interesting. A blush spread across her cheeks as she fidgeted.

"I might have run a search on all of you," Nikki said, but she looked at RJ.

RJ nodded. It wasn't like he hadn't done the same.

"You did what?" Dylan asked, his voice even and low.

Uh oh, Dylan isn't going to like the invasion of privacy.

She shrugged. "Do you blame me?" she asked. "I needed to know if you were trustworthy."

"Then you ask me," Dylan demanded. "Or go to Cameron. You don't stick your nose where it doesn't belong."

"Well…" RJ held up his hand. "I sort of did the same thing to them."

Dylan snapped his hard gaze over to him and stared at him for several moments then sighed. "Of course you did."

"That doesn't explain why you approached RJ," Brandon pointed out.

Now that the subject had been brought up, RJ was curious as well. Nikki could have gone to Ben today, but instead she'd been in his shop.

"I figured anyone with a record like his had to be moral."

"Record?" RJ asked.

"Your military file," she explained.

"My missions are classified," he said slowly. There was no way she'd be able to get that kind of information.

"Yes," she said. "But if you know the right people, you can still get some of it. Anything that had to do with names, places or national security was blacked out, but I had enough to form an opinion on what kind of man you were."

RJ could only stare at her. *Fucking unbelievable.* "No," he said in horror. The details in those files were something that he didn't even want to read.

"I'm sorry! I had to know," she exclaimed.

RJ stared at Dylan for some kind of help. Words were just not coming to him.

Dylan held up a hand. "Maybe we should skip over this right now."

Brandon nodded. "Yeah, I don't think I want to know what laws my sister broke." He glanced up at her. "I know you're doing what you think is best, but you've been here two days. You can't just come in and fix things."

"Why not? No one else was doing anything."

"This is bigger than just our family." Brandon ran a weary hand over his face. "Even if I don't challenge, I know someone will," he muttered.

"Can I ask a question?" Ben asked from the couch where he and Justin had settled. "Who approached you to challenge?"

"I can't...I can't tell you. It wouldn't be fair to him."

"But it's fair to let him pressure you to challenge an appointed Alpha?" Nikki questioned.

"Let's start this way," Dylan offered from across the

room. Everyone peered over at him and he smiled. "Let's address the issues one at a time. First, I support the shifters going public."

Brandon shrugged. "I see both sides of the argument. But I guess I have been lax in supporting it, so that is what's brought up the most. And I don't honestly think that is what this is about. I think they're using it as an excuse. They're more worried about losing the ear of the Alpha. Especially when you decide on your own inner circle. That will leave a lot of us out in the cold."

"Okay." Dylan leaned forward. "Cameron had agreed to go public, and when I accepted the Alpha position, I kept the agreement. I have also discussed my inner circle with Cameron and he has agreed. You can't tell me that Cameron would have been challenged."

"No, I don't think so," Brandon conceded.

"So what else is the problem? Me being a stranger? Cameron spoke to several of you, from what I understand, about bringing in an outsider."

"He did," Justin spoke up. "To all of his inner circle plus several of the younger wolves who were dominant."

"Did he contact the elders of the community?" Dylan asked next.

"Not until he'd decided on you," Brandon answered.

"Now, I'm not trying to get out of you who approached you, but I would bet it was one of the elders. Maybe an elder who's worried that if you don't challenge me, his own son will," Dylan guessed.

RJ stared at his brother, open-mouthed. What in the hell was Dylan talking about? Or who?

"So you know?" Brandon inquired.

"I suspect," Dylan corrected. "The reason I've been spending so much time with Cameron is because I'm learning about all of you that I will be answering to. See, that's the difference to being an Alpha, in my opinion, from some of the elders. I don't believe the Pack is here to protect and work for me. That's my job. To make sure we flourish and remain safe at all times."

Brandon inclined his head.

"I haven't told Cameron about the rumors. I've been hoping I could take care of it. I made a mistake," Dylan admitted.

RJ didn't like hearing Dylan sounding so defeated. "Dylan—"

"No," Dylan interrupted. "I should have been spending more time with the Pack. There's just been so much to do and a short amount of time to learn about the people who'll be under my protection."

"I haven't been looking at things from your point of view," Brandon said.

Finally, the lines of communication were opening up. RJ was beyond relieved.

"I appreciate that," Dylan said. "I want to work with you and the Pack. I don't expect a perfect transition, but I am becoming Alpha. A challenge won't change that."

"I wish everyone thought that way," Brandon said.

"I understand it being hard for you. I don't think pushing you into the challenge is the right thing to do, though. You obviously care about these people. Can you say the same about them?"

Nikki gasped. RJ figured she knew who their brothers were talking about. He wished he had a clue. "You can't protect him forever, Brandon. I know he used to be your best friend, but he's not the same kid you grew up with," Nikki told her older brother.

"I know." Brandon sat. "I know."

The room fell silent. "Have you tried talking to him?" Nikki asked, after a pause.

"Yeah, couple of weeks ago. He won't listen to reason. His father's not helping. That old man should have been put down years ago. He's not happy unless he'd making someone miserable, usually his son." Brandon peered around the room. "I wasn't born to lead, I know that, but I don't want to see my Pack split in half, either."

"I don't want to see that, either. It's not only me, but my family and my friends. I want this Pack to be strong and grow. I want everyone to be happy," Dylan stated, with conviction.

"So now what?" Brandon asked. "I won't challenge you." He reached out to take Nikki's hand in his. "I can't do that to my family. But that doesn't make the problem go away."

"Then let's figure out what will," RJ suggested.

Brandon glanced at him. "Sorry I punched you. I haven't been thinking clearly lately. The thought of you using Nikki to get to me had me seeing red."

"No problem," RJ replied. He grinned at Nikki. "We could have probably come up with a better plan than ambushing you both, but we were running out of time."

"Yes, you could have," Dylan said. "And I'm pretty sure I told you I would handle this."

RJ laughed. "True, but did you really expect me to listen?"

That had Brandon chuckling. "We may have to watch the two of them together. I can see nothing but trouble in our future."

Nikki huffed. "Whatever."

"I think we need something stronger than coffee," Ben stated, standing. "Not that I ever brought it in."

"A beer sounds good," Dylan said.

"Yeah," Brandon agreed.

"Beers all around," RJ declared.

"Can you help me?" Ben asked Justin.

"Sure," Justin agreed.

As they left the room, Nikki moved and sat next to RJ.

"Good work," he whispered. Dylan and Brandon would both be able to hear them, but RJ didn't care. Nikki had stood up to and for her brother. The time had come for the Pack to do the same.

"Now comes the hard part," she responded. "Actually figuring out what to do."

"I have some ideas on that," Justin announced as he returned with three beers in his hand.

"I do as well," Ben added.

RJ accepted the cold brew from his brother and tilted the bottle at him. "About time you pulled your weight," he teased.

"Well, now let the smart brother talk," Ben quipped. "Maybe you'll learn something."

* * * *

The plan was simple. So simple it might *just* work. Get everyone involved who would support them and spread the word that the Pack needed to stick together and support Cameron's decision. Cameron and Dylan went to the diner for breakfast before walking the around town together, Nikki wrote articles for the paper to publish the next morning. RJ would speak to the new Pack members, asking them to mingle with the older members, and Justin talked with the kids at the school and in his shifter classes. Hoping the support of the Pack and bringing everyone together prior to the ceremony would calm the waters, they all worked hard to do their best.

Once Nikki had turned in her special edition article, about her hope for the future under Dylan and her support of the Cross family, she walked out of the newspaper office and headed downtown. She was lucky that the editor of the paper hadn't had a problem with her plan. Since he was related to Cameron and good friends with her brother, Nikki had felt confident approaching him with her idea.

She waved at Sabrina and Max, who were posting flyers about the pre-ceremony barbecue on shop windows. Ben had come up with the idea of getting the Pack together before instead of just after the ceremony and Nikki thought that was brilliant. The youngest Cross brother had turned out to be smart as a whip…and, if she wasn't mistaken, taken with her own sibling, the middle child. Justin had been sending sly looks Ben's way also. It would be fun to see where that went.

Her own attraction to a Cross brother was a little more of an issue. Brandon still suspected something was going on and, in all honesty, there was. Even though they'd all been up late working out who would do what, she'd managed to find herself backed against a wall with RJ's tongue in her mouth once again. She'd been coming out of the bathroom and when they'd passed he'd grabbed her.

Nikki hadn't wanted to get away, either.

Which would probably explain why she was walking toward his shop. Since they'd separated, she hadn't been able to stop thinking about him. Nikki crossed the street a few stores from RJ's tattoo shop. He stepped out, holding the door open as another man walked ahead. The stranger was shorter than RJ but had the same muscular build. His hair was buzzed and the Marine Corps tattoo down his left arm that matched RJ's had her figuring this was one of RJ's military buddies. RJ glanced up when she got to the sidewalk and the smile he sent her was so bright her breath caught. *God, he's handsome.*

"Hi," she greeted.

"Hello there," he replied. RJ ran his gaze over her and Nikki felt somewhat embarrassed. There was no question that he appreciated what he saw. She liked that about RJ. There was no playing games needed, just like the previous day when they'd kissed, RJ was not making excuses for finding her attractive. "Miss me?"

Then there's his smart mouth. Nikki wanted to shut him up with her lips. And there was nothing to stop her. She grabbed a hold of his T-shirt and yanked him forward, laying her mouth over his lips in a sweet, deep kiss.

RJ slipped his arm around her waist, tugging her up against his body.

The strong hold felt damn good. She pushed her tongue along his.

A throat-clearing broke the sexual haze and she pulled from RJ but didn't look at the stranger yet.

"I needed that," she whispered across RJ's lips.

"Well, honestly, I'm not gonna complain about that." He turned her toward the stranger, who grinned from ear to ear. "This is one of my best buds. Mike Jackson," he informed her. "Mike, this is Nikki Stratton."

Mike held out his hand. "It's nice to meet you."

"You, too." Mike was a good-looking man, but Nikki preferred her biker. She peered up at RJ. Too bad his friend had decided to visit. Nikki had been ready to see if she could tempt RJ into a make-out session before she had to meet her brother. "I finished my article. It'll be in the paper tomorrow."

"We're heading over to the café for lunch. Join us?" RJ asked.

Nikki glanced at her watch. She needed to meet Justin in an hour. "Sure, I have time."

They started down the street receiving several smiles and a few waves, even. Some were from her old Pack members and others from people she didn't know.

"Is this usual for you?" she whispered to RJ.

He swung a casual arm over her shoulder. "No, never. Either we're making progress or it's the calm before the storm."

Nikki hoped the reactions meant good things. "So, Mike, where is your Pack?" she questioned RJ's friend.

"Northern California. I haven't been visited in a couple years. The last mission...made me miss it, though," Mike admitted.

RJ stiffened.

"What?"

"We haven't talked about what you might have read in my file that you shouldn't have gotten access to," RJ said.

Yeah, she hadn't thought last night would be the end of that conversation. "You did the same thing," she defended.

"I didn't break into classified information!" RJ pulled her to a stop in front of the café door. "There's stuff in there that I don't want anyone to know." He looked at Mike. "Right?"

Mike held his hands up and took a step back. "I don't

think—"

Nikki slapped his chest. "This isn't the time or place to discuss this. People are watching and we're supposed to be getting along."

"Is that so?" he almost growled.

"Yeah I—"

She was lifted off her feet so fast that she didn't have time to brace herself. Instead of finding herself face to face with an angry RJ, Nikki was kissed, deeply and thoroughly. *Fuck, if he keeps moving his tongue over mine like that, I'll lose control and begin humping him in front of a café full of people.*

"Well, looky here, boys. Nikki Stratton has returned and is playing in the gutter."

RJ set her down and she whirled around to face the speaker. Her back was pressed to RJ's chest, which could very well end up being a good thing, as she couldn't see this interaction going well.

"Samson," she greeted him in her best polite tone. She nodded at his two friends. "Will, Body, how's it going?" If she could keep everyone calm, maybe they could get out of this without bloodshed. It hurt to see the man she'd once been close enough with to consider a brother so bitter and acting ugly.

Samson sneered. "Didn't your brother teach you any better than to hang out with trash?"

She gripped the bottom of RJ's shirt when he moved past her. Nikki managed to stop him from charging Samson, but they both knew Nikki wouldn't be able to hold him off if he really wanted to get at the guy.

"You got a problem, man?" RJ snarled.

Mike darted a little to the side and straightened his shoulders, bracing his feet. RJ vibrated in fury next to her. Crap, they didn't want a brawl in front of the café the day before the party to unite the Pack.

"Yeah, I got a problem. You. You and your brothers." Samson's lip curled.

Nikki stepped between Samson and RJ. "That's enough.

Why don't you just keep going, Samson?"

He snorted. "I see where your loyalties are. Brandon knows about this?"

"Why? You gonna tattle on me?" she challenged. She wasn't afraid of him. Brandon and Samson had been best buds until they'd reached high school. After that time, Samson had changed, turned into a bully and Brandon had spent less and less time with him. "Don't forget, Samson, I grew up with you. I know all your secrets, too."

Samson shook his head. "Bran's always been too easy on you, should have turned you over his knee. Maybe I'll do that myself."

RJ surged forward. "Touch her. I dare you."

Samson's eyes narrowed. "You think I'm scared of you? I'll touch who I want."

To prove his point, he grabbed her left wrist. She managed to hold off RJ with her right, but barely. It was Mike who moved the quickest. He had Samson's free arm up and angled. Samson hissed.

"Why don't you just let her go?" Mike suggested, his tone level and calm. "You really don't want to do this here."

Samson released her and turned on Mike. "You'll regret that."

Mike scoffed. "Get out of here, man. You're making a scene. Just go and get control of yourself. Sober up some. I can smell the alcohol on you."

Samson brushed past them and headed off, cursing them and making threats. Nikki looked up into the wide café windows and saw several tables of people staring at them.

"Damn it," she muttered and dropped her head.

"Asshole," RJ grunted, still watching Samson as he crossed to an old Chevy truck.

"Hey." She yanked RJ forward by his belt loops. "Let it go."

He frowned and twisted his neck. "He fucking put his hands on you."

She held up her wrist. "And I'm fine. But now we have to

go eat and make sure we show a united front."

He glanced up at the café. "Shit. That was him, wasn't it? The one that Brandon is trying to protect."

"He wasn't always like that. At one time he'd have thrown himself in front of a speeding car to protect me."

"This isn't going to end," RJ said. "He was more than drunk. I could smell some chemicals, too."

"I didn't realize how far gone he'd grown. If he challenges Dylan, he won't win," she said.

"That's why they're trying to pressure Brandon." RJ threw his arm around her shoulder and herded her to the café door with Mike following behind. "I can't believe your brother used to be best friends with that dick."

She sighed. "My second year in college, they had a final falling out. Bran never told me what about, though. I didn't think it was my place to push." Now she regretted that decision. Brandon had to know Samson wasn't going to make it much longer if he didn't get help.

"Well, let's try to enjoy our lunch," RJ suggested, opening the door.

There was still a fire in his eyes, but she let it go. It would be a long day.

Chapter Five

Nikki pulled up at the old bar at the edge of town where she'd promised to meet RJ. They still had some time until Brandon got off work and Dylan finalized things with Cameron. The next night would see if their last-minute efforts were going to do them any good. She still needed to tell Brandon about her encounter with Samson earlier. Justin had been pissed, but he'd understood why she wanted to wait to tell Brandon.

If Brandon went after Samson for touching her, which was a good possibility, there would be trouble sooner than the ceremony.

She didn't see his Harley, but Nikki needed a drink. No one would mess with her there, anyway. They might be on the outskirts of the city limits, but she was still the sheriff's sister. She parked her Jeep and stepped into the warm night air. Even at ten in the evening it had to still be in the eighties. At least there wasn't the humidity that she'd never gotten used to in Houston. No, this was a dry heat. This was home.

The music played low and the smoke was thick when she opened the doors. Not too many people were there at this time of night on a Monday. She ignored the four men playing pool and walked to the back booth where her date waited. Not that this was a date. Or maybe it was. She didn't have any idea. RJ smiled and slid out of the booth after she reached the table.

The kiss she received was just shy of erotic and had her toes curling. It seemed he really didn't care who saw them together. She'd made the first move, kissing him in front of his shop, but his move in kissing them in front of the café had garnered them much more attention. All through lunch she'd felt people's eyes on them but hadn't picked up on any hostility. A few women that she'd gone to high school with had even stopped by her to say hi. Of course they'd checked out RJ and Mike the entire time, but Nikki had been amused.

"I'll get you a drink. What's your pleasure?"

She nearly said he was but swallowed it at the last minute. "Light beer on tap."

He nodded and guided her to the seat he had just vacated.

She put her purse beside the wall and watched as he walked to the bar. He wore tight black jeans that cupped his ass perfectly. RJ cocked his hip on the bar as he ordered, surveying the room. When two beers were set in front of him, he pulled out his wallet and paid then turned to her.

His white shirt stretched tight against his chest. She hadn't gotten to see him naked yet and if that didn't happen soon she might go insane. Things would have been so much simpler if they'd met back in Houston. Nikki would have taken him to bed and enjoyed several hours before sending him on his way and getting on with her life. In Lawton, things worked in a different way. There were no such things as random hookups in a small town. Going down this road with RJ wasn't smart. Not only were their brothers barely tolerating one another, but they'd be thrown together at every Pack event from here on out. At least when she came to town, which brought about another worry.

It wasn't until she'd been back with her brothers that Nikki had realized she might not have made the best decision leaving, as she'd always believed. She'd missed seeing them all the time. Nikki hadn't even realized that she'd been lonely. Sure, she had friends and some were even shifters, but no one she had a bond with like her brothers. No man she'd shared the type of connection that was forming with RJ. Last week her life had been much simpler.

RJ smiled sweetly at her; joining Nikki on her side of the booth. Nikki scooted to give him more room, but in response, he closed any distance she'd made. Okay, not that she minded having his hard body against hers, but she didn't want to attract too much attention from the other patrons.

"So no one overhears us," RJ said, with a wink.

Nikki didn't buy that innocence for a second. "Better for them to think we're hooking up?" she asked.

He chuckled, the deep sound tickling her senses. "I think we both know there is more going on here than hooking up."

"I…" Nikki wasn't sure how to respond.

"Did everything else go okay?" he asked, changing the subject.

"Yeah," she told him, relieved. Nikki wanted RJ, there was no doubt about that, but the complications were just so many. "Talking to Justin's fellow teachers and students, we realized that the group that wants a challenge is pretty small. I don't think Samson or his friends know that the majority of the Pack are fine with Dylan taking over. The improvements to the economy, schools and revenue are a big deal to most."

He sighed. "I'm glad. I haven't spoken to Dylan yet, but Ben says the same thing."

"Hopefully my article in the paper tomorrow morning will reach anyone we might have missed." There couldn't have been a lot of the residents who hadn't been contacted that day. They'd split up on reaching out. Nikki still didn't understand why no one had thought about doing so earlier.

"When we meet up with Dylan and Brandon, we should have a pretty good idea if they foresee any issues."

Nikki nodded. "What about your friend? Is he still here?"

"He's at the house with Ben," RJ replied. "I wanted to spend some time with you alone."

"Really?" She blushed. Nikki liked that RJ just said what he felt, although it would take some getting used to. "Why?"

"I think we discussed the Pack issues enough for now," RJ stated. He slid his hand under the table to her knee. "It's time to talk about us."

"Us?" she squeaked. He palmed up her leg toward the hem of her skirt.

"Drink your beer," he said, nuzzling her neck.

Nikki picked up her glass, trying to ignore her shaking hand. She wanted to feel his lips on hers. Hell, she hoped he continued to run his fingers higher up. There had been a reason that she'd worn a skirt instead of pants. Not that Nikki had expected to have his hand halfway up her thigh. But she had wanted to show off more of her body. So far he'd only seen her in jeans. Nikki took several sips until she couldn't stand it any longer. She set her beer back on the table. Her mouth was only inches away from him.

"Kiss me," she pleaded.

He grinned seconds from slamming his mouth on hers.

Nikki might not have been kissed a lot in her life, but she had no doubt that RJ was the best at it. He leaned in with his whole body while thrusting his tongue over hers. She grasped his shoulder when she grew dizzy.

RJ pulled away. "We should probably get going. The things I want to do to you shouldn't be done in front of a bar half full of people."

"Yeah," she breathed out.

"Unless you're into that kind of thing," he whispered. His found the edge of her panties with his fingers.

"I'm not." She spread for him anyway. He teased her over the thin material of her panties. Nikki was already wet for him. "RJ, please."

"Come on!" He grabbed her hand and pulled her from the booth.

She laughed and stumbled as he continued to drag her through the bar. They hit the door and ran out into the night.

"Where are you parked?" he asked, lifting her off her feet.

She held on to his shoulders and wrapped her legs around his waist. "Who cares?"

He chuckled as he walked farther from the bar. "I see it."

She was busy kissing and biting at his neck so she didn't very much care if he found the car or not. Just the taste of him was breathtaking. His salty skin called to her.

"Baby, if you keep that up we aren't going to make it to the Jeep."

"Uh-huh," she murmured. Really, all that they needed to do was get to a flat surface. She wanted him inside her this time. She squeezed his waist and he groaned. She went back to sucking at his neck. Nikki grunted when her shoulders hit the side of her Jeep.

"You drive me crazy," he told her then devoured her lips.

She slid lower, rubbing across his hard body. "Want you...please...need you," she managed when they broke away to breathe air in. This was insane, but she was past caring. She'd think about the consequences later. Right then, she just wanted any part of RJ she could get.

"Christ." He glanced around the empty parking lot while opening the passenger door and pushing her inside.

She giggled as she fell into the seat.

"Gonna be quick," he warned, leaning over her and pushing her shirt up.

"Don't care," she promised, already starting to unsnap his jeans.

They managed to move their clothes out of the way enough so he pressed up against her. Nikki was already panting. It wasn't going to be long for her, either. Already her clit tingled from the slight pressure of his jeans across her.

"Look at me," he demanded, just inches from taking her, his cock hard and pulsing at the lips of her pussy.

She lifted her head. His eyes held the power of his passion and she shivered. "RJ, now!"

He thrust inside, going deep with the first thrust. Her breath caught and she clawed at his back. Perfect—what she needed.

"Oh fuck, you feel good," he managed, pounding into her.

She tightened around him and lifted her hips to meet each wild, passionate plunge. This was what she craved, what she'd longed for on those cold lonely nights. Someone to take her. Someone to swamp out all her feelings and just demand a response. "Yes! Yes!" she cried as he rode her hard. Nikki ran her hands over every inch she could touch—his head, his shoulders, chest and stomach. The ink on him rose and shimmered when they moved.

"Mine, all mine." He spoke each time he buried himself inside.

She heard him talking but couldn't concentrate on the words. The feel of him inside her, the sight of the pleasure on his face and the fierceness in his eyes was mesmerizing. The pressure built until she couldn't stand it.

"Almost!"

He grabbed her face and their eyes locked. "Now," he growled. He snarled, throwing his head back, and slammed inside.

"Yes!" she cried again as she exploded. Her orgasm tore through her body. She clutched at him, pulled, tried to anchor herself.

RJ paused long enough to watch her, but as soon as she slumped down into the seat, he withdrew his cock, nice and slow, only to thrust in. The intense need might have been sated, but Nikki wasn't quite finished with him. She squeezed her inner muscles to clamp down on him, drawing out a growl.

"Harder," she demanded. "I want to feel you later."

"Christ," he mumbled but complied. Each fierce drive shook the vehicle. "Gonna." He came hard, filling her with his seed. Nikki hugged him close when he dropped his head beside hers. RJ tilted his face and kissed her neck. "Stay there."

"Okay," she agreed. Like she actually wanted to move. Her bones felt like jelly. Nikki wasn't certain she could stand if she needed to. No one had ever made love to her with so much passion.

RJ drew out of her gently before grabbing some napkins from the dash. He dabbed at what had to be his cum leaking from her body. "Do we need to talk about not using protection?"

She shook her head. Shifters couldn't carry or pass on human STDs but there was still the issue of pregnancy. "On birth control."

He growled.

"What?" That hadn't been the reaction she'd expected. Shouldn't he have been relieved?

"I don't like the thought of you with anyone else." RJ had no trouble looking her in the eye as he spoke.

"Oh." That aggressive, dominant side of him was arousing. "I haven't been with anyone for a while. I'm picky."

"Are you?" RJ straightened as he asked. "I'll count myself lucky."

Nikki pushed on his chest to move him. She needed to right her clothes. Someone could come out of the bar any minute. It had been stupid to give in to their lust in public, but she also couldn't stop smiling. RJ appeared very pleased with himself as he yanked up his jeans. It was cute.

Once Nikki was decent, she peered around the parking lot. "Where's your bike? I didn't see it earlier."

"I had Mike drop me off. Figured that I could catch a ride back to the house with you. We are going to the same place, after all."

She nodded. It was probably close to them being late. "I guess I could give you a lift. You'll owe me, though."

He slipped his arm around her then yanked her hard to him. "You can start a tab."

Nikki didn't waste any time closing her lips on his. She would never get tired of kissing him. RJ tugged himself away. "Our family is already going to know what we were doing. We probably don't want to be any later."

Yes, scent didn't lie and she would have RJ's all over her. Justin wouldn't say anything, but Brandon had already voiced his displeasure at her interest in RJ.

She walked around her Jeep to the driver's side, letting RJ climb into the seat he'd taken her in. Nikki would never look at the passenger side the same way again.

Once they were both buckled in, she started the car and shifted into drive. RJ remained quiet but the wide grin hadn't left his face. If their brothers didn't know from the scent, they'd be able to figure out what the two of them had been up to just by the look on RJ's face.

"Stop smiling," she ordered.

"Who me?" He put his hand to his heart. "I have no idea what you're talking about!"

"You so don't manage the innocent act."

RJ laughed. "I damn sure do."

"I never imagined you'd have this childlike glee in you," Nikki commented.

"Dylan would agree with you. It drives him nuts."

Nikki laughed. "I can only imagine how much fun it was growing up at your house."

"It wasn't bad," RJ confirmed. "My parents have always traveled and luckily the rest of the Pack looked out for us. Pretty much Dylan was always the responsible one."

"So he sort of raised you and Ben?"

"You could say that. It wasn't like with Brandon and you, though. My parents made sure we had plenty of money, but they weren't so great at the love and affection part of parenting. Dylan more than made up for it."

"So he'll be a good Alpha?" Her question was quiet and she wondered if RJ heard the hope in it.

"He'll be wonderful," RJ stated with confidence.

"Good."

RJ kept Nikki's hand in his as they walked up the steps to his house. Voices in the living room were a mere soft rumble while he led the way through to the den. He had to smother a grin when he walked in and saw Justin leaning close to Ben on the couch. RJ could have given the two guys some privacy but he wasn't that nice of a brother.

"Hey, guys." He watched in amusement when they jumped apart. Nikki smothered a laugh and he had to hold in his own.

Ben blushed and dipped his head. Justin, looking a little more comfortable, just sighed and leaned back. "Great timing," he muttered in complaint.

Nikki brushed past him and patted his head. "Better luck next time," she teased.

Justin wrinkled his nose. "At least one of us got something."

This time both Nikki and Ben blushed.

"Where's Mike?" RJ asked.

"He planned to work out then shower before everyone got here," Ben replied.

"Giving the two of you time alone?" RJ teased.

"Shut up, RJ!" Ben pleaded.

"Hey, I thought I heard voices," Dylan said, joining them.

Everyone froze in place. Dylan walked halfway through the room. "What? What did I miss?"

Nikki cleared her throat, Ben squirmed in his seat and Justin found his hands interesting.

"Okay, what?" Dylan asked again.

"Brandon's not here yet. I'll put the coffee on." Ben jumped up and ran out of the room.

Dylan raised an eyebrow and glanced at him. RJ just shrugged. He wasn't going to give Ben away. Ben would tell them when he was ready. Besides, it was fun knowing something that Dylan didn't.

"Hmm," Dylan hummed. "Okay, you want to tell me about your run-in with Samson Lewis in front of the café instead?"

Damn. RJ rethought throwing Ben under the bus but just couldn't do it. He strolled over to his spot on the fireplace hearth, where Nikki had already taken a seat.

"He started it." RJ didn't know how else to explain.

Justin tried to hold in a chuckle and failed. Nikki slapped a hand on her forehead while Dylan scowled at him.

"I know you did not just say 'he started it' like a four-year-old," Ben commented, returning to the room.

RJ thought once again about telling on his younger brother but that really would have made him look like a four-year-old. "Well, he did," he complained.

Nikki elbowed him as she addressed his brother. "We were walking to the café when Samson came out and made some...rude comments."

Dylan leaned forward and nodded. RJ sighed. His older brother was not going to accept that small of an explanation. Dylan could be like a dog with a bone sometimes. Especially when it had to do with something RJ didn't want to talk about.

"Normally, you wouldn't lose your cool over some words. You have better control than that," Dylan stated, his tone saying he knew there was more.

RJ wanted to squirm in his seat like Ben had earlier. "Yeah, well..."

"What did he say, RJ?" Dylan asked, short and to the point.

"He was talking about me," Nikki told them. RJ noticed she was also rubbing the wrist Samson had grabbed.

"And?" Dylan pressed.

"He put his hands on her!" RJ exploded and stood. "And had we not been dealing with this damn challenge, I would have taken him out."

Dylan raised his hand. "And you would have been right, but there are ways to handle things. What would have happened then?" Dylan asked.

"I would have fucked up what we are trying to accomplish with the Pack," RJ admitted.

"Which was his point," Dylan assured him.

"I know that." RJ plopped down and accepted Nikki's hand when she held it out to him. He kissed her palm, which calmed him a bit. "I did find out something else, though. He is in no condition to challenge you. He'd been drinking, heavily, and is in no way as strong as you," RJ told him.

Dylan nodded. "That's why they needed Brandon." Dylan glanced at his watch. "Who should be here by now."

"I'll call him." Justin pulled out his cell phone.

"So, if they've lost Brandon, does that mean they won't challenge?" Ben asked from across the room.

Dylan shrugged. "I don't know. Cameron tried to get hold of the elders but no one would answer. We couldn't find them around town either. They've shut him out."

Nikki groaned. "I don't understand why they are trying to stir everyone up. There's only, like, six of them left. They don't even hold any positions in the Pack anymore."

"But they're still listened to and they advise Cameron. I think they're worried about losing that small amount of power," Dylan noted.

"Straight to voicemail," Justin informed them, slipping his phone into his pocket. "If something came up around town he'll take care of that first. You know how he is."

Nikki nodded. "Probably lost track of time."

Mike appeared in the doorway. "Sorry I'm late."

"Don't worry about it," RJ said. "We're still waiting on Brandon."

"I talked to him about an hour and half ago," Mike said. "He was getting ready to head over."

"I hope nothing serious came up," Ben stated.

"I'm sure it's fine." Justin patted his arm. "Brandon is hardly on time for anything."

Both Cross siblings laughed, which helped RJ relax.

"So, is everything set for tomorrow?" Dylan changed the subject.

"The food will be there in time. Toby, from the café, volunteered to man the grills with help from some of the others. Steve, over at the church, is taking the tables and chairs they use for their parties. I'll meet with him to get everything set up," Ben told them.

"I'll catch up with Ben along with some of the older teenagers. They'll help us get everything done," Justin added.

They heard a car door and waited as Brandon walked in and joined them in the living room, still in uniform. Brandon nodded to Dylan. "Sorry I'm late, but something came up."

Everyone remained silent at his somber tone.

"RJ, man... I'm sorry. Someone broke into your shop and tore it up pretty bad."

RJ jumped to his feet before the others could even react.

"RJ, wait!" Nikki grabbed hold of his arm. He tried to shake her off, but she held firm. His shop? His new baby? Fury rushed through him.

Brandon blocked his way. "I know you want to see, but I need to ask you a few questions first."

RJ shook his head. "No, we all know who did this." He looked at Dylan. "This was Samson. I should have suspected he'd try something like this."

"We'll find out for sure," Dylan said, taking charge. "You and Nikki go ahead with Justin and Ben and head over. I'll ride with Brandon and explain on the way. Mike?"

"I got my bike," Mike said, already striding to the front door.

"Now wait just a damn minute!" Brandon barked to the whole room. "I'm the sheriff and I have some damn questions!"

RJ could feel his wolf close to the surface. He wanted to find that coward Samson and smash his face in. He rolled on the balls of his feet in preparation for jumping around the sheriff. He didn't give a damn what the man said. He wanted to go, now.

"Brandon." Dylan's voice was calm "Let RJ go. I'll explain everything."

Brandon sighed but waved a hand. "It's a crime scene so don't go in without me," he cautioned.

RJ nodded and, as gently as he could, grabbed Nikki's hand to pull her with him. He didn't care if Ben and Justin caught up or not, but he wasn't letting Nikki out of his sight after this. If Samson went after him, he'd be spineless enough to try something with her.

Mike had left the front door open and was already on his bike, revving up. RJ wanted to take his own motorcycle, but with his emotions high and his wolf clawing to get out, it wouldn't be safe. He had to make sure Nikki didn't get hurt.

Justin hit the key fob on his SUV, making the lights flash. "I'll drive."

RJ let Nikki maneuver him into the back seat while Ben jumped into the passenger side. The doors had barely closed as Justin took off. RJ appreciated that the other man was hurrying. Energy pumped through his body and only the fact that Nikki was rubbing his arms and legs kept him calm at all. He'd worked so hard to achieve his dream of having something that belonged to him.

"I'm sorry," she whispered, kissing the base of his neck.

He closed his eyes and took deep breaths. "My last mission was the rescue of the feline Prince Zachary," he started.

A gasp came from the front seat, but Nikki just took his hand and gave it a squeeze.

"His cousin knew that Zach had mated with another cat—a bobcat who ran the unit I was in—and our departure ended up as an opportunity," he explained. "Prior to leaving for the mission, Casey asked a favor of me. I'd done all of the unit's tats, but he wanted a special one for him and Zach. He wanted matching mate tats so that, when he wasn't with his mate, he could always see him." He opened his eyes and pulled her close. "I drew their mate in cat form on each other's chest. Zach's lion over Casey's heart and Casey's bobcat over Zach's. They were the most important pieces I ever did."

"That's wonderful," she told him, running her hand over his throat to grab his chin. "I can imagine how important that was for them. Especially after Zach was taken."

He nodded, glad she understood. "That's what I want to offer. That tattoo kept Casey sane while we were searching for Zach. He had his love with him in some way."

"We don't know how bad the damage is," Nikki said. "No matter what, we'll get you back on track. Trust me."

"I want to rip his fucking throat out," RJ grumbled.

"He won't get away with it," she promised. "He'll pay for this."

"Actually, he's going to pay for more than just this," Justin said. "He's been playing Brandon for years and you haven't told the rest of us what happened this afternoon, but touching my sister is not going to be something I let go."

Justin sounded so fierce that RJ saw a new side of him. Justin might appear soft-spoken and calm but there was a protective instinct strong within him.

"Everyone just needs to stay calm." Ben, as always, ended up being the voice of reason. "Dylan and Brandon will figure out something. We should just concentrate on the shop."

RJ growled. He wanted to go one-on-one with Samson. Samson needed to learn not to fuck with the Cross family.

Justin pulled up in front of RJ's shop and it was both too soon and not soon enough. There were several people outside in the street and on the sidewalk beside the tape the sheriff department had put up. The windows were all busted up and the door was smashed.

"Fuck!" RJ cursed under his breath.

"Hey," Nikki murmured, blocking his view. "It's going to be all right."

RJ knew it would, but this hit deep. It'd been the only thing he'd wanted when the unit had decided to retire.

"I'll be here with you," she promised and kissed him one more time.

And that was the best thing he'd ever heard. He'd already gained so much more than he had thought. He had a new home, his brothers back, loyal friends and Nikki. He wouldn't have even imagined finding her. He hadn't been looking. But there she sat, worrying and upset, because he was.

"Yes, it will," he declared, staring into her eyes. "Better than ever."

"That's the spirit," she teased him. "You needed a little more color anyway."

"Did I?" he asked, smiling. He knew that she was attempting to mess with him to take his mind off the damage.

"Some pink," she stated.

"I tried to tell him that," Ben said from the front seat. "He was all about black leather."

"What?" he asked. "I like the smell."

Nikki leaned closer to whisper in his ear, "I can't wait to take a ride on your bike. Do you have any leather chaps?"

And just like that RJ's cock stirred to life.

"Of course I do," he admitted.

"Mmm," she practically purred.

"You know we can hear you," Justin complained.

"It's not like I described how I plan on peeling them off of him," Nikki said. "I could go into great detail about being on my knees when—"

"Stop!" Justin shouted.

"Yeah." RJ took her hand and pressed it to his straining erection. "I would like to actually try a bed next time. Not another vehicle."

"TMI, bro!" Ben said, groaning.

RJ laughed. They managed to help him push past the anger.

"Are you ready?" Nikki asked.

Was he? It might hurt to see what had been done to his shop, but at least it remained standing. Things could be a lot worse. He nodded and slid out of the vehicle behind her.

Chapter Six

Nikki didn't know what to do as a look of pure despair crossed RJ's face. Mike broke away from the other spectators on the sidewalk and embraced RJ and she appreciated that he did. She was beyond pissed off that this had happened. RJ had only been targeted because of her. He'd threatened Samson in order to defend her. If she hadn't been with him that afternoon, RJ's shop would still be in one piece.

She didn't understand why Samson had changed so much. Yes, his father was a bit of a prick, but Samson had always stood up for himself. He'd spent a lot of time with the Stratton family. To this day, Nikki still wanted Samson to return to the caring teenager he'd been. *It can't be too late. There are redeeming qualities.* She just didn't know how to reach him.

Staring at the glass that littered the sidewalk, she doubted herself. With Samson's drinking and drug use, it was going to take more than just talking to him to get him back to who he'd been. And people could get hurt in the meantime.

She sighed. RJ's vision for his shop was meaningful and, out of the blue, a tattoo of her mate in his wolf form leaped into her mind. She eyed RJ. It might be way too soon to even consider RJ as a mate, but the thought stuck there. As much as she flew around the world, it would be nice to have a connection with home like that.

Maybe not now, but she'd have to think about it when and if she ever returned to Houston. Nikki was lucky enough that she could be based anywhere. The travel assignments were issued over the phone, and being in Lawton she could still do her job.

Years ago she'd been searching for freedom. *Now what do I want?*

"Nikki?"

She turned toward RJ. He looked puzzled. Damn, she'd gotten lost in her own thoughts when she should have been taking care of RJ. He held out a hand and she quickly clasped it, letting him pull her close.

"I don't want you going anywhere without me or Mike with you," he said once she was against him.

Huh, what have I missed? "Excuse me?" She glanced up at him. *Where the hell did that come from?*

"Just listen." He turned and cupped her face. "This is a direct attack on me. Add in that your brother has switched sides, and Samson's words earlier... I don't want you alone." Mike was beside him, nodding.

"RJ, this is my hometown. Everyone knows me and I have been on my own a long time. I have been in more hostile places than this. I can take care of myself."

"Just wait until after the ceremony," he pleaded. "If something happened to you... I wouldn't be able to hold in my wolf. I need to make sure you are protected."

She opened her mouth again to protest when Justin interrupted, "I agree. You're a target now. All of us are. You shouldn't be alone, either, Ben," Justin added.

Ben frowned. "Now wait!"

"Enough!" Mike growled. "It goes for everyone in both families. No one from either family will be alone. Double up and figure it out."

"I couldn't have said it better," Dylan offered as he and Brandon joined them. "In fact, Brandon and I just spoke about the same thing in the car on the way over."

Nikki shook her head, but she knew she was beaten. She might have been able to fight against RJ and Justin, but just the expression on Brandon's face told her he was in full protective mode. "Fine."

Everyone else agreed and Brandon put a hand on RJ's shoulder. "I'll take you inside to but don't touch anything yet."

RJ clenched his jaw. He nodded and glanced at her. "Come with me?"

She offered him the best smile she could manage. "Of course."

"I'll take Mike and get some wood to cover the windows and door," Dylan said. "Ben, you and Justin hang out here and watch everyone. Samson might not be here, but I doubt he wouldn't have eyes and ears out to let him know what's going on."

Nikki kept a hold of RJ's hand as Brandon led them inside. On top of the windows and door glass having been smashed, all the furniture had been upended, the leather couches and chairs shredded, ink spilled over the counters, floors and walls and RJ's instruments had been broken and tossed around the shop.

"Son of a bitch," RJ grumbled. "Damn it!"

Nikki rubbed his arm with her free hand as he took in the mess.

He stomped over to the floor where several pages of paper were ripped up. Nikki squinted, trying to figure out what it was.

"My sketches," RJ said, his voice quiet.

Jesus, did they have to tear up his work?

"You have insurance?" Brandon asked from the door.

RJ nodded. "Yeah, of course. Ben made sure everything was in place."

"Okay, I'll give you a copy of the report as soon as I can."

RJ turned with an expression of rage on his face.

"Listen, man," Brandon said, holding his hands up. "We didn't start off on the best of terms. That's my fault, I can admit it."

RJ tilted his head.

"I'll make up for my behavior and it'll begin with helping you rebuild."

"You don't have to do that," RJ said.

"Maybe not, but this sucks. It's a clear violation and a

challenge, but we need to handle this legally."

"*Legally*," RJ repeated.

"We can't go vigilante on Samson. It will send the wrong message to the Pack. You're the new Alpha's brother."

"I hate this," RJ declared.

"I know. Let me handle this, RJ. It's what I do and I am damn good at my job. But what we *can't* do is let this distract us, let him separate us and what we are planning to do about mingling the Pack."

RJ growled and picked up one of the chairs before hefting it across the room.

"Feel better?" Brandon deadpanned.

"Bran!" Nikki complained.

But RJ started to laugh. "Actually, I do."

Nikki glimpsed between the two of them as they both chuckled. She threw her hands up. "Men!"

"However, I do need to ask you not to touch anything else," Brandon stated. "We're going to do a full investigation. I have one of my deputies outside ready to take fingerprints."

"When can I get in here?" RJ asked.

"In the morning," Brandon said. "I just need a few hours."

"Then what?" Nikki pressed. "Are you going to arrest Samson?"

"I need proof, Nikki."

"Proof?" she demanded. "Come on! We all know he did this."

"He did it the night before the ceremony, expecting a strong reaction," Brandon stated. "We need to be calm here and let things play out."

She snorted. *This is fucking ridiculous.*

RJ wrapped his arm around her shoulder. "I hate to admit it, but Brandon's right. This is just a distraction. If we go after him, he'll use it as an excuse against Dylan. The ceremony is tomorrow night. We'll get the shop cleaned up and I'll reopen. But after Dylan is Alpha. All of our attention needs to be on the ceremony."

"Fine," Nikki said. "But we're all helping you in here."

"That works for me."

"And we will replace that furniture right away."

"Furniture?" he asked with a raise of an eyebrow.

"So we can break it in properly."

"Nicole!" Brandon objected as RJ grinned.

She laughed and started for the door. "The sooner we get this place boarded up, the quicker we can start...practicing."

She wasn't surprised when RJ beat her to the door while Brandon mumbled, following. Nikki wouldn't under normal circumstances be so vocal about a relationship within earshot of her eldest brother, but this was about making RJ feel better. That and she really did plan on helping RJ break in his new furniture. She was also starting to get a thing for black leather.

Outside, Justin and Ben stood in the street, blocking the view of anyone hanging around as Dylan and Mike kneeled with supplies.

"What's going on?" RJ asked, crouching.

"The men with Samson earlier are across the street. We're trying to figure out how to go after them without drawing attention to ourselves," Mike said.

"No!" Brandon growled. He, too, dropped down. "Let my department handle this."

"We're not going to talk to them. Just see if they go and report to Samson," Dylan stated.

Brandon sighed. "Mike, you're the one who isn't known well. Can you slip away and get behind them? Follow when they leave the scene?"

"I can," Mike assured him. "I'm trained in this. Just give me the right opening to disappear and I'll get it done."

"Good enough," Brandon said. "Please don't make any contact with them."

"I promise," Mike said. "They'll never know I'm following them."

"Okay — let's get these windows covered and Mike can do his thing," Dylan said.

RJ helped Dylan lift one of the large boards. Nikki

followed with a hammer and nails while Brandon and Mike grabbed another piece. She didn't know how Mike was going to sneak off, but she made it a point not to look in his direction. She didn't want to give away anything to Samson's buddies.

"Just relax," RJ whispered.

Nikki nodded. *Relax?* That was easy for RJ to say. He'd been involved in more serious situations than this.

"Nikki." RJ snapped his fingers.

"What?"

He smiled. "He's already gone. Just act normally."

She glanced to the side and saw Justin holding up the board with Brandon as Ben hammered nails in. "Oh." *Guess I don't need to worry about giving Mike away.*

* * * *

RJ groaned at the loud beeping in his ear. He reached over and slapped the alarm off before burying his head into the pillow.

"It can't be morning already," came the complaint from next to him.

RJ lifted his head and grinned. Nikki lay wrapped in his bedspread with her head hidden under the pillow. He'd taken her home with him the previous night and they'd spent all evening into the early morning hours practicing how they would 'break in' his new shop furniture. He chuckled while scooting closer to edge the top of the blankets down, revealing her naked shoulder. He ran his tongue over her soft skin until she shivered.

"Ugh!" she said; laughing. "You can't want more already."

RJ smiled. He was actually feeling pretty sated but just waking up beside her had all kinds of ideas popping in his head. "Well, if you can't handle it…"

The pillow above her head slid off the bed as she burst up. "Can't handle? *Me?*"

He chuckled. "Well…"

She pushed herself up and crawled along him, causing him to roll over. She straddled his hips and bent low, her hair curtaining them. "Well what?"

"Oh, nothing," he said, as much innocence in his tone as he could manage.

"Hmm." She brushed her lips across his. "Feeling better?"

He smirked and raised his hands over his head. "Feeling pretty damn good."

"Oh really?"

"Yes, as matter of fact…" RJ sucked in his breath when she grasped his cock under the covers.

"You're right, baby," she teased. "You do feel pretty damn good."

He sucked in a breath and she tightened her grip and rubbed her body down his.

"As a matter of fact, you feel so good I think I'll have to taste."

He did his best not to buck with her wet mouth wrapped around his shaft. But damn, did she have a talented mouth and that thing she was doing with her tongue…

"Baby…" He buried his hand in her hair. "More."

She looked up at him from between his legs and deep-throated him again.

"Oh, sweet Jesus!" he yelled, unable to keep quiet.

She continued to suck and lick until he at last lost control and plunged in and out of her mouth. She urged him on with a hand on his hip.

"So good… Yeah, suck me deep… Oh, baby…"

Too soon, his climax threatened. He tightened his hold on her hair and gave a gentle tug. She popped off and grinned.

"Get up here," he ordered, already pulling on her. "I don't want to come until I'm inside you."

She moaned, sitting astride his thighs. "Yes."

He held her around the waist while she positioned herself over him. She sank down slowly, drawing a moan from them both.

"God, you fill me so good," she told him, arching once he

was seated deep inside her.

He couldn't have agreed more. He held her tight and pushed his hips up. "Come on, baby, ride me."

She pressed her hand down on his shoulders and rose before sliding down. She took her time, rising and falling, teasing and taunting.

"Please, Nikki," he begged as she tortured him.

Her laugh was wicked.

He slapped her ass playfully. She tightened around his cock and moaned. *Oh, now this is interesting.* He did it again and was treated to her gasp and her pace picking up.

"Yeah, baby, faster, harder," he encouraged and gave her another smack.

"RJ," she cried, tightening even more.

He braced his feet on the bed and thrust up each time she came down on his cock. They sped up, with him spanking her every few strokes, until only the sound of flesh against flesh filled the room.

RJ lifted up to sit and gripped her hips hard, yanking her down on his shaft deeper. "Come for me, Nikki, come on my cock."

She did. Crying out his name, she fell over the edge, pulling him with her. He dropped down, keeping his arms around her as he struggled to catch his breath. She nuzzled his chest and he knew he wanted to wake up like this every morning for the rest of his life.

Pounding on the door broke up the peaceful, sated state he had fallen into.

"Come on, you two! Get your asses in the kitchen," Dylan ordered.

Nikki groaned.

"We're coming!" RJ called out to his brother.

"God, I hope not!" Dylan shouted. "I'm surprised you haven't killed each other yet."

Nikki squeaked and started to squirm off him. RJ tightened his hold. "He's just messing with us," RJ tried to assure her. He wasn't ready to lose the connection with her yet.

"No, I'm not! If you two go at it again, I'm going to make you sleep in separate rooms," Dylan argued.

"Damn shifter hearing," Nikki muttered. "The horrible thing is Brandon would be just as bad."

"I know you did not just compare me to your brother," Dylan called. "How about I get him on the phone and he can see if he can get you two out of there?"

That got Nikki moving. She leaped off the bed in a flash.

"We'll be down in a minute!" RJ hollered, watching a blushing Nikki dart into the bathroom. His brother's laughter started to drift away and RJ rubbed his hand over his face. He'd have to think of a way to get him back and soon.

It was about time that Dylan settled down. In fact, RJ didn't know of any serious relationship that his older brother had been in. Dylan had always been the love-them-and-leave-them type. Now that he was Alpha, it wouldn't be as easy for him. Not unless he casually dated one of the humans in the towns close to him or a shifter from another Pack.

Dylan had already stated that he wouldn't be with a shifter from their Pack unless he was prepared to settle down with her. Too often Alphas found themselves the center of attention just because of their position.

The shower turned on and RJ climbed out of bed. If he wasn't able to join Nikki, he could at least get dressed so he wouldn't be tempted to bring his brother back there. He wouldn't put it past Dylan to get Brandon over to embarrass Nikki further.

* * * *

After a wonderful, if not embarrassing, morning, Nikki found herself with Justin and Ben at the Pack clearing, getting ready for the barbecue prior to the ceremony. She was pleased with the number of volunteers who had come and the progress they were making.

Six grills stood off to the side ready to be fired up. The

teenagers of the Pack had finished setting the tables and chairs and started piling wood in the fire pits for later in the night. She grinned as Sabrina and Max began to load one of the tables with an assortment of desserts. It was all coming together. They just had to get through the night and hopefully by morning they would have a new Alpha and the Pack would be complete. Then she would have to figure out what she was going to do about her and RJ.

When she'd made the trip home, she hadn't known anything about what she had now found herself in the middle of. Finding a man like RJ hadn't even been on her radar. Now she couldn't imagine returning to the city without RJ. But she could tell that RJ was at home here — with his brothers, with his Pack — and she couldn't ask him to leave. *So where does that leave us?*

"Penny for your thoughts," Ben said, his voice soft as he came up behind her.

She turned and smiled at the youngest Cross brother. "Do you think we'll be able to pull this off?" Okay, that wasn't what she had actually been thinking, but it was close.

Ben looked around and nodded. "I think so. Even if Samson tries something, without Brandon there to back his play I don't think much can come from it. The Pack respects Brandon and that was our biggest concern. He would have support just because he'd earned it. Samson doesn't have that going for him."

"Brandon never wanted to be Alpha," Nikki reminded him.

"No, he didn't. But if you hadn't come down, I don't think we would have been able to come together like we did. All Dylan and Brandon needed to do was relax and talk about the future of the Pack. To see that they both shared the same ideas on our future."

Nikki laughed. "Yeah, well, leave it to the men to be stubborn and almost fight instead."

Ben chuckled and Justin caught her eye as he moved from the group of teenagers to talk to Max. She glanced over at

Ben.

"So you want to let me in on what's going on between you and Justin?" she teased.

Ben blushed and shifted on his feet. "Uh...well..."

Nikki turned to face him with a smirk. "Should I ask what your intentions are with my brother?"

Ben shook his head, his eyes going wide. "No! It's not like that! I mean...we haven't really decided..."

She threw an arm over his shoulder and turned them so they could see Justin trying to steal a cookie from one of the platters an older Pack member placed on the table. She slapped at his hand, but he danced away, laughing.

"Just treat him right. I think the two of you are perfect for each other."

Ben sucked in a breath. "Really?"

Nikki hugged him closer. "Yeah."

"I've never felt like this," Ben confessed. "He makes me laugh. Makes me feel like there might be something besides work to concentrate on. He's just so friendly and free."

"He is good at that. I think he became a teacher both in school and for the Pack because he can relate to them so easily."

"I like him," Ben confessed.

"Make sure he treats you right. I'd hate to have to kick my brother's ass."

"Speaking of kicking a brother's ass, may I ask why you are hanging on mine?" RJ's voice came behind them.

"Because he is so damn cute!" she told RJ as he pulled her away from his brother and into his arms.

"Not cuter than me, though, right?" RJ asked and winked.

"I...I think I'll go see if Justin needs some help," Ben gabbled and left them alone.

Nikki didn't even glance after the other man. Her entire focus was on the one in front of her. "I wouldn't really say you were cute," she taunted.

"No?" he breathed against her neck.

"No. Sexy, maybe. Hot, for sure."

"Mmm, sexy, I like that," he told her, licking a path from her ear down her neck.

"Oh yeah, sexy as sin." She shivered when he started to nibble.

"Haven't the two of you had enough of each other yet?" Dylan asked as he joined them.

RJ sighed and loosened his hold. "I hate you."

"You don't mean that."

"I might not if you would stop cock blocking me," he groused.

Dylan laughed. "My sympathies."

"Where's Brandon?" RJ looked around. It had been agreed that Brandon and Dylan would partner up for the day so that neither man would be alone.

Dylan nodded to the parking lot. "He's going over something with his deputies. He wants everyone on high alert. Hopefully the ceremony will go off without any problems, but I don't see Samson just giving up. That attack on your shop last night shows how pissed he is."

"Hey, where's Mike?" Nikki asked RJ. Mike had been supposed to stay with RJ for the same reason.

"He had some calls to make. I left him in the truck."

A commotion from the parking lot had them stiffening up. Nikki let out a nervous laugh when a dozen small school-aged children came running into the clearing.

"Damn," Dylan groaned, rubbing the back of his neck. "We need to calm down or we'll have heart attacks and the ceremony hasn't even started."

"No shit," RJ said. "We're too jumpy. If we can't control ourselves, the Pack is going to pick up on it."

"So what do we do?"

"Act as normally as possible even as we stay aware of our surroundings." RJ kissed the side of her neck before pulling Dylan by the arm. "Come on, brother. Let's get a drink."

Nikki watched them go, smiling. They stopped to talk to several people, both new and old Pack members, finally making it to the drink station. She saw Justin and Ben sitting close together at a table off to the side.

"I never thought I would see you smiling at someone like that here at home."

Nikki turned to face Brandon. "I didn't either," she admitted. When he didn't say anything else, she figured she had some things to tell him. "You know I was pissed when you ordered me home?"

He nodded. "Yeah, you didn't hide that well." Brandon led her away from the others. It appeared he needed to say a few things to her as well. Nikki didn't like that this seemed to be the only time they had serious conversations—when something bad might happen.

"I'm sorry for being such a little shit," she said.

Brandon laughed. "Nothing to apologize for."

"Still, being here this time has me thinking a lot about the past. You didn't have to do everything that you did. We weren't really your responsibility."

"I don't regret a thing."

"That's good. I really am very lucky. Justin, too."

"Have I ever told you how proud I am of you?"

"Yes, I know," she assured him.

"I read every article," he said. "It scares me to death to know you go to some of the most dangerous parts of the world. It also makes me feel as though I didn't do too bad a job raising you."

"Or Justin," she added.

"Yes," he agreed. "But I never worried about him the way I did you. I guess I always knew it would be you that would try to take on the injustices in the world."

Nikki laughed. "Just like you have to protect everyone."

"Turns out Justin *is* the smart sibling," Brandon said. "He's the only one who chooses to stay out of danger."

"Nah, he's just crazy."

Brandon raised an eyebrow.

"Kids?" Nikki said. "Teenagers, to be more specific? You have to be nuts to choose that profession."

Brandon chuckled. "Someone has to do it."

"I guess." She gave a mock shudder. "Better him than me."

"Damn." Brandon smiled. "It's good to have you home."

"What would have happened if I hadn't come?"

Brandon shrugged. "I hope I would have gotten my head out of my ass. I got caught up in all the politics."

"You have it worked out now?" she asked, stepping closer to her brother. He was a good man, so she did believe he would have figured it out. No matter what happened, she was proud of him.

"Dylan asked me to be his Beta. He wants Max and RJ as his Enforcers and a couple others from both Packs in the inner circle. Everyone he named made sense and Cameron agreed with his choices. I do believe he will make a good Alpha."

"Well then, congratulations," she said with a hip bump against him.

He grinned. "Thanks, but it's not over yet."

"We don't even get to celebrate a new Alpha or your promotion. Samson has taken that from us."

"I know."

"You never told me what happened between the two of you. Why you stopped being his friend," Nikki said.

"It doesn't matter," Brandon said, his voice small.

"I think it matters to you," Nikki corrected. "You stopped being his friend, but you never gave up on him."

Brandon sighed.

"You can tell me," Nikki pressed. "Maybe it will help."

Her brother was silent for several minutes then nodded. "You know his dad is an asshole."

Nikki snorted. *That's an understatement.*

"Samson loved coming over to our house because he felt like a part of the family. He'd get hell when he went home, but he always told me that a few hours with us was worth whatever his dad did to him," Brandon explained.

"What changed?"

"Sarah Green."

"Your ex-girlfriend?"

"Yeah, I guess he had a crush on her, although he never told me. When I started dating her, Samson was supportive. Over time he turned bitter. And started to talk to her behind my back."

"He tried to steal her away," Nikki guessed.

"The sad thing is had he told me, I would have broken up with her. I wasn't in love or anything. She was just a girl who I took out sometimes."

"Then what happened?"

"He stopped hanging out with me and got mixed up with the wrong crowd. Began doing drugs. Took Sarah with him."

"Oh, God!" She regretted asking. The pain in Brandon's voice made her ache to comfort him.

"She got addicted to meth," Brandon said. "Eventually she overdosed."

"Shit." Nikki hadn't heard about any of this. She'd met Sarah a few times and had known that Brandon wouldn't ever mate her. Nikki just hadn't picked up on any sort of strong connection. "I'm so sorry."

"When I confronted Samson, he just shrugged off his responsibility for what had happened to Sarah. I knew he was messed up, too, but I couldn't do it anymore. I couldn't watch him destroy his life."

"I'm sorry."

Brandon shook his head. "I've tried to get him into rehab. To get him help. I've even clashed with his father over it."

"If he doesn't want to get better then there is nothing you could do."

"I know," Brandon agreed. "But he was my best friend."

So much made sense. It hurt that Brandon had dealt with this on his own. "Justin doesn't know?"

"Not all of it. I didn't want him to get involved."

Nikki didn't know what to say.

"Now that you know what's been going on, you shouldn't have to be told to be careful. Samson isn't thinking straight.

If you get in the way, he'll hurt you. Don't think you can reason with him."

"I won't," she promised.

"Stay close to either me or RJ."

Nikki sighed but he cut her off.

"I mean it. This will be the last chance before anything done against Dylan will be against the Alpha. It's all or nothing tonight."

"I know, Bran," she assured him. "I'll be careful."

He nodded. "Cameron just arrived. I have to go over a few things with him."

He left. She'd gotten more out of him than she'd expected. Nikki glanced around the yard, pleased at how many of the Pack were already showing up. With the ceremony still several hours away, it was a good sign.

At least something is going according to plan.

She had a feeling that Brandon didn't believe this would work. He expected trouble, which meant that she needed to be alert.

RJ waved her over to where he stood with several Pack members. She plastered on her best smile as she strolled over. She'd have to fake a good mood even if she was scared to death of what the night would bring. It wasn't just her own family who were in danger anymore.

In the span of a few days she'd started to care about the Cross family, one in particular. If Samson had something up his sleeve, she wouldn't be able to relax until she returned home and all of this was over.

Chapter Seven

RJ felt the excitement in the air. The Alpha ceremony would start soon and the Pack was in full celebration. Cameron, Dylan and Brandon stood in the middle of the clearing, preparing for the circle. Justin and Ben were working the crowd like pros and Nikki was in the middle of a group of women around her age. They laughed and squealed and he couldn't hold in a smile as she shook her hips and danced away, laughing. He caught her eye and the look in hers changed, moving from happy to heated with passion. He jerked his head to the edge of the crowd and she nodded.

The pre-gathering had gone off with no problems. Samson hadn't even shown up. The closer the time to begin came, the more RJ relaxed.

Maybe our efforts have actually been enough.

"How're things going?" he asked Nikki when she reached him.

"Good," she replied with a smile. "Everyone I've talked to seems ready and willing to accept whoever Cameron puts in place. Dylan has some of the older ladies eating out of his hand already and the younger ones"—she laughed—"are asking if he's mated."

"Dear God!" RJ said then groaned, not sure if his earlier thoughts of his brother taking a mate had been wise. As much as he wanted his brother happy, he wasn't looking forward to some of the women trying to win his brother over. There'd probably be females all over the place, always dropping by the house. RJ was going to need to stay at his small apartment over the shop if that happened.

"I know." She sounded gleeful. "It's going to be so much fun to watch."

The way she spoke, it sounded like Nikki planned to be around. They hadn't yet talked about their future and RJ hoped she was, but the ceremony was taking everyone's focus. Eventually the two of them were going to have to discuss what was going on between them.

RJ wanted to explore their relationship further. Nikki appeared to want the same.

Something in his gut screamed at him that things wouldn't be simple, though.

"What's wrong?" Nikki placed her palm on his elbow, drawing his attention from his thoughts.

RJ shook his head. Now was not the time. This was his brother's day. RJ would have tomorrow with Nikki. "Nothing," he said. "Just thinking."

Nikki narrowed her eyes.

"Nikki!"

They both turned as a couple of teenagers came running up.

"Casey! Erin!" Nikki cried, opening her arms for the girls. "Wow, you've grown up so much!"

Nikki almost fell over from the force of the hugs she received. RJ placed a careful hand on her lower back to help steady her without getting in the way.

"Oh, my God!" the peppy blonde said. "I can't believe you're here. It's been forever!"

Nikki grinned and patted the girls. "Well, I couldn't miss this. Tonight is a big deal for the Pack."

"I know, right?" the redhead stated. "Isn't the new Alpha hot?"

"He's not bad," Nikki responded. "Have you met his brother?"

Both girls paled as RJ stepped forward.

"Oh, my God! You're the biker!" the blonde said.

RJ laughed. "I am."

"This is Casey," Nikki said, running her hand over the

long blonde hair. "And Erin." She nodded to the redhead. "I babysat them when I was in high school."

"She was the best!" Erin declared. "We got to write and act out plays and skits. My mom still says it's your fault I want to be an actress."

RJ grinned but felt a little tinge in his heart. He wanted to be a part of Nikki's past. It was ridiculous, really. How could he feel jealous of a babysitting job? Still, RJ felt that strong a connection to her.

"Ladies and gentlemen, Pack members." Cameron's voice rose above the crowd. "It's time."

"Go find your parents," Nikki ordered the teens. "We'll catch up later. Make sure you stay close to them, no matter what."

"We will!" Erin promised while dragging her sister away.

"It'll be okay," RJ had to try to assure her. He shouldn't make that promise, but he hated seeing how she'd tensed up.

"This is it," Nikki whispered. "If Samson or anyone is going to challenge it'll be now." She peered around the clearing. "There are so many innocent people here."

"Justin, Ben and Mike will get them all away if there are any problems," he reminded her.

"What about Dylan?" she asked.

"He can take care of himself," RJ said. "Dylan is meant to be Alpha. I have no doubt in his abilities."

Nikki blew out a deep breath. "I hope you're right."

He did, too. Sure, he believed in his older brother, but RJ also never wanted to see Dylan hurt. Any challenge, even one Dylan won, would take a toll on him. RJ wouldn't be able to help, either. All challenges were one on one.

"Please join me at the circle as we welcome our new Pack members and begin the Alpha ceremony," Cameron invited.

"Come on." It was going to happen. Dylan would be marked as the Alpha. RJ led Nikki around and through the crowd until they stood next to the circle beside Brandon,

Justin and Ben. Dylan kneeled in the middle of the circle with his head bent.

"Woodrow Wilson once said, 'The ear of the leader must ring with the voices of the people'. I have tried to listen to each member of this Pack and always advise with all of your best interests in my heart. My time has passed and another's has begun."

RJ looked at his brother with pride almost bursting from his chest. Nikki slipped her hand into his and gave it a squeeze. The feelings of happiness threatened to overwhelm him.

"I know in my heart that my replacement will be able to lead the Pack in the right direction and protect you as the shifter world moves forward with plans on going public."

There was a stirring behind Cameron, but RJ's view was blocked.

"The future of the Pack will rest on the shoulders of this man. I want each—"

"Excuse me, Alpha Cameron!" someone shouted from the crowd.

No, fuck! RJ strained to see around the people in front of him. Pack members shuffled around while Samson led a small group forward to stand at the edge of the circle across from them. Samson was backed by some of the elders and their families and a half-dozen men he'd never seen.

There was a gasp in the crowd and he heard the murmur of words like 'feline', 'cats' and 'shifters'.

RJ searched for Mike and saw him moving forward. Dylan rose as Brandon stepped to his side, showing his support for the new Alpha. Justin and Ben had begun to already push several of the Pack away. There was going to be trouble and everyone knew it. RJ glanced down at Nikki's pale face.

"You and Ben go with Mike," he whispered to her, waving a hand at the man.

"RJ, no!" She gripped his hand tighter.

"Please."

Mike arrived to pull Nikki back. She fought, but a glare from Brandon had her grumbling but going into the crowd. RJ didn't want her too far from him, but he trusted Mike to ensure her safety. After Samson's actions in front of the diner, he didn't trust the asshole not to go for Nikki.

RJ made his way to his brother and the others in the circle.

"What is the meaning of this, Samson?" Cameron demanded and faced the other man. RJ, Brandon, Justin, Max and a few others fanned out behind him and Dylan.

"You have your pick for the future and we have ours." Samson motioned to one of the big strangers next to him.

Samson's father was grinning widely, almost bouncing as well. RJ wondered, not for the first time, what in the hell was wrong with that family. They couldn't actually expect to have approval for a different species to lead the Pack. That was insane.

"You have no authority to choose the next leader. I am Alpha and the choice is mine," Cameron stated, bracing his feet apart and standing to his full height. While aged, the man was still a powerful force.

"You just said you listen to your Pack," Samson challenged. "Your Pack has a different vision than you."

Cameron took his time peering around his Pack. All of the Pack members who had already been at the ceremony had separated from Samson, leaving a wide area between them. "I believe the majority of the Pack respects my wishes."

"But not all. This is a Pack decision, one that will affect us for many years." One of the elders spoke up from behind Samson.

"So, instead of following my choice, you bring forward a man, a feline shifter we know nothing about?" Cameron inquired with a nasty twist of his lips.

"Fred been in charge of his small group of felines for several years," Samson argued. "He is just as qualified as Dylan Cross."

There was more rumbling in the crowd, but Cameron held up a hand.

"What exactly do you suggest?" the Alpha asked.

"Simple. A challenge. Dylan and Fred. Winner takes Alpha position."

RJ went to step forward, having heard enough. There was no way he was going to let his brother fight some feline they knew nothing about. Dylan shook his head at him. RJ was going to ignore his brother when Brandon gripped his shoulder.

"Dylan needs to handle this," Brandon murmured.

RJ shook his head. *This is unbelievable. They have a problem with Dylan leading so they bring in a cat shifter no one even knows? Dylan's been in town for months, getting to know his new Pack.* And it didn't matter what anyone said—RJ was not convinced that the fight would be fair.

"I accept the challenge," Dylan stated, his voice strong and rich over the crowd.

"No!" Ben cried.

RJ agreed with his brother. "Absolutely not. How can we even ensure it would be a fair challenge? There is no one here to judge the feline," he protested.

"It's a good thing I made it in time, then," another voice rose from the crowd.

RJ turned and saw the members of his military unit standing with Mike, Nikki and Ben. The Prince of the felines stepped forward. RJ knew his mouth was hanging open but *holy shit!* He was so fucking relieved to see his best friends.

"I believe I am able to judge the challenge fairly. I also have the ability to take down one of them if they choose to use means not approved for the challenge," Prince Zachary announced.

Activity picked up when everyone recognized the power of the strongest cat in the world. Cameron nodded and waved the Prince forward. RJ met the gaze of his friend and the Prince's mate, Casey Williams. He cut his glance to Nikki in silent meaning. Casey looked surprised then smiled. He nodded and placed his hand on her shoulder. RJ knew Casey would protect her.

Prince Zachary stood tall, peering out of the crowd. Samson was whispering frantically in Fred's ear. Fred's stance had changed and he appeared uncertain. *Jesus, I'm lucky someone called in my team.* RJ hadn't wanted to bother anyone with his problems and that could have cost Dylan his life. RJ needed to do something to help protect Dylan now.

"Ten minutes to prepare," Prince Zachary called out.

RJ walked with Mike, Brandon and Justin to Dylan and pulled him aside. There would be a challenge and he'd be damned if he was going to lose his brother. He would give the man every single piece of information he had learned over the years of fighting next to the cat species. Some of his best friends were felines, but this was a fight he wouldn't let his brother lose. He just hoped Dylan knew what he was doing.

"Are you sure about this?" RJ asked Dylan.

"If I don't accept, we'll have trouble in the Pack. I can't risk anyone else getting hurt," Dylan responded.

Brandon sighed. "Which shows why you are the perfect choice for Alpha. I feel like an idiot for the way I acted."

Craig, the Prince's guard and RJ's good friend, walked over with a smile. "Do you mind if we have a word?" he asked Dylan.

Dylan glanced at RJ, who nodded. Craig was small but deadly. The feline guard had the toughest job in the world, protecting the Prince.

"I'll see what I can do to help," Mike offered, walking off and taking Brandon and Justin with him. RJ wasn't going anywhere.

"What are you doing here?" RJ asked.

"Mike called. Asked if we wanted to come see your new town and maybe hang out. He had a bad feeling," Craig explained.

"So did I, but I didn't expect this," RJ replied.

Dylan snorted. "This never even crossed my mind."

"Have you ever fought a feline?" Craig asked.

"No," Dylan answered. "The only felines I've even met are you guys."

It was a good thing that RJ had brought his team around his brothers once in a while.

"The strength of wolves comes with the Pack. Fred doesn't care about anyone here around him. You have support and you need to use that to your advantage," Craig stated.

"A challenge is one on one," Dylan said.

Craig smiled. "Close your eyes."

Dylan frowned, looking shocked. "What?"

"Trust me." Craig nodded. "Close your eyes."

RJ didn't know what Craig was doing and gasped in surprise when Dylan complied.

"Concentrate on those around you," Craig whispered. "Do you feel your Pack? Your territory?"

They were silent for several moments.

"Yes," Dylan said with awe evident in his voice.

"You might be alone in the circle when you face off against Fred, but that doesn't mean you don't have the Pack behind you. They need you to be their leader. Don't let them down."

Dylan blinked his eyes open. "How did you know that would work?"

Craig laughed grasping RJ's shoulder. "Felines make Packs, too, although our instincts are different." Craig glanced at him. "We made a Pack from the team."

RJ dipped his head in agreement.

"It's not natural, but it can be done. In battle we depend on each other. The bond is what helped us make sure everyone returned."

"Wow," Dylan murmured. RJ was also a little taken back. He hadn't realized that during his time in the service he'd made his own Pack. It made sense now that it was in the open, but RJ had just followed his instincts. Knowing that the felines had felt the connection had him grinning.

"That means I consider RJ's Pack as my own as well," Craig said. He squeezed RJ's hard. "We'll discuss you not calling us later. You should have contacted us when you had Mike."

RJ dropped his head. He expected to catch shit from all his team mates. He'd screwed up.

"He'll be fast, but you have the link to the Pack, your family and the land. Watch his teeth. That will be how he'll try to take you down," Craig told Dylan.

"Got it," Dylan said.

"Spend some time with your brothers before we start," Craig suggested. With a hug for both of them, he then walked away.

Ben came running over and embraced Dylan. RJ turned to face both of them. Dylan grabbed the back of his head and dragged him down into the three-way hold.

RJ took a deep breath to calm himself. If Dylan was going to use his connection to the Pack in order to win, then he'd pick up RJ's full support the entire time.

"Thank you for being here," Dylan whispered.

Ben took both of their hands. "We're a unit, brothers, family. You remember what you're fighting for."

"I will," Dylan promised.

RJ had to clear his throat before he could speak. "We love you," he told Dylan. "So you'd better fucking kick this feline's ass."

Dylan laughed.

"Does anyone know what he is?" Ben questioned.

"Tiger," Brandon said, walking up to join them.

RJ was glad that Brandon had come in full support of his brother. He peered around until he spotted Nikki, surrounded by his team. The stark look of fear had him wanting to console her, but RJ needed to be there for his brother.

Casey leaned down to speak to her and she pressed her lips together. Finally she nodded. Oh, she was going to give his fellow soldiers a run for their money. They'd never met a female like Nikki. RJ was also going to enjoy every minute of it.

Nikki couldn't believe all the activity around her. Parents of young children were asked to take them home and anyone who didn't want to witness the challenge had been given permission to leave. It didn't surprise her that most of the Pack had stayed. This would affect them all.

She wasn't sure of the finer details of Samson's plan, but Nikki knew it wouldn't be good. Bringing in an unknown feline shifter to lead a Pack of wolves? It was beyond crazy. The years of drug use had to be affecting his decisions.

The arrival of the Prince of felines and RJ's old military unit couldn't have come at a better time. RJ had appeared just as surprised to see them, so Mike must have been the one who'd asked them there. Nikki didn't care who'd made the decision — she was just thankful for it.

However, the immediate protective circle they'd made around her was irritating. She could be doing something right now. There were still kids and teenagers hanging around and they didn't need to see what was going to happen. Every time she tried to pass, one of the men would politely block her path.

"If you'll step over here with me, we'll take our place now," the man who had introduced himself as Casey asked.

She pressed her lips together. Nikki wanted to be at Brandon's side, next to RJ. This was her family, too. "I don't..."

"Please," Casey said. "This fight is going to be vicious and it'll be easier for your brother and RJ to watch out for additional trouble if they know you're safe."

"I could help," she stated.

"Yes." Casey grinned. "I have no doubt. Still, I'd feel better if you stood by me. My mate is going to be right in the middle of things and I'd appreciate your help in keeping an eye on him."

She followed with a sigh to where she would still be able to see but where there was no one behind them. "Your mate is the Prince?" she asked.

Casey's entire face lit up by his smile. "Yes. Isn't be sexy?"

Nikki laughed. The Prince was not bad, but she preferred the roughness of RJ's appearance. "Hmm," she murmured, still eyeing RJ's muscles.

"Oh, I see," Casey teased. "You like them big and bumpy. I prefer my sleek man."

Nikki moved her gaze to the Prince, where he stood speaking to Cameron. The Prince was good-looking, no doubt. He was tall, with a swimmer's build.

"Don't be getting any ideas." Casey wagged his finger at her. "He's completely taken."

"I'm being kept plenty busy as it is," she responded with a wink.

"Oh! I'm so going to like you," Casey stated.

She smiled, but it was quick to slide off her face when Dylan stepped up into the circle. Samson remained by Fred's side as he took his stance across from Dylan. Nikki had really been hoping that a challenge wouldn't take place once Brandon's decision had been made. *Samson couldn't actually think that a feline would be able to take over as Alpha.*

"This is wrong," Ben whispered, grabbing her hand.

"I know." She held on tight.

Cameron and Prince Zachary stood between the two fighters as the others backed off to give them room. RJ crossed his arms over his chest, directly across from Samson. She knew her man was taking that spot on purpose in case Samson tried to pull anything against the rules. That put RJ in a dangerous position. Samson sneered at RJ, but the way he darted his eyes around revealed some of his worry. That had once been Brandon's best friend. She still remembered the times he'd shared dinner with them, helped her with her homework.

Fred was bouncing on his toes, shooting glances between the Prince and Dylan.

It was obvious that the arrival of the Prince had been a shock to them. Nikki just hoped it would keep the challenge legal and fair. Everyone knew that the Prince would have no problem bringing either man down if they cheated, but what about the damage before that?

The challenge started without any ceremony. Cameron and the Prince waited until both men had stripped and shifted then they backed out of the circle.

The tiger roared, but Dylan just lowered himself to the dirt and growled. Saliva dripped from Fred's teeth and she shivered. Those were lethal weapons. If the tiger pierced any of Dylan's vital spots, Dylan could be killed at once.

Nikki had never seen anything like this challenge. Dylan in wolf form was impressive. He was fully black and big. However, the tiger was huge. The feline swiped at the wolf, who just darted out of the way. *Okay, so Dylan's quick — that's good.*

The two animals came together with a clash of fangs and claws. Nikki had to close her eyes several times as the fight continued. The sound of bone-crushing hits and the sight of blood spraying was just too much to handle. Ben started to shake beside her and she wrapped both arms around his waist to hold on to him. Their guards stepped even closer to them. A good fifteen minutes of pure battle had to be wearing them out. Nikki was ready to collapse and all she was doing was watching.

Dylan bit at the tiger's neck while the massive feline claws scraped down him. All attention was on the two fighters, so no one noticed Samson until it was too late.

Samson shifted and howled then launched himself at RJ outside the ring. RJ only had enough time to cover his face landing on the ground with the wolf on top of him.

"No!" Nikki screamed and started toward him. She was caught around the waist and lifted off her feet. She kicked, yelling to be let go. This was what she'd been afraid of.

"Don't," Casey ordered, holding her tight.

Nikki panicked. The other cats who had arrived with Fred started to shift and so did the wolves with RJ. Brandon, Justin, Max and even Mike. RJ still fought to hold Samson off so he could shift himself.

"Do something!" she yelled at Cameron and the Prince.

"We can't," Prince Zachary told her, his face revealing regret. "As long as they don't cross into the circle, they are not interfering with the challenge."

RJ managed to get away from Samson long enough to start stripping off his clothes. Mike lunged at Samson but was blocked by a cougar protecting the wolf.

Inside the circle, Dylan growled out a warning as another two felines tracked RJ's shift. As soon as he was in wolf form, they attacked. The distraction worked for the felines. The tiger was able to pounce on Dylan and pin him down for several moments. Luckily, Dylan managed to avoid the powerful jaws, but only just.

Nikki didn't know where to look. Both of her brothers, the man she loved and her future Alpha were all battling while she could only watch.

"Let me go! Let me go!" she demanded, digging her nails into Casey's arms. She had to do something. Her entire world was being threatened and her wolf was raging inside.

"Don't shift," Casey ordered her. "Hold on. RJ needs all his attention. If he has to worry about you, it could cause him to get distracted."

Nikki knew Casey was right, but she just couldn't hold it in. Her body shook with the effort to contain her animal. It had never been so hard for her to stay human. The sounds of tearing flesh and the scent of blood were not helping at all.

RJ took a hard blow, knocking him back. Brandon leaped to cover RJ until her lover was back on his feet.

"Calm down," Casey urged. "It will be okay. Just breathe. Deep, long breaths. RJ is trained for this. He's faced worse odds and always comes out on top."

"Go help," she ordered. Her voice was deeper than normal with her wolf so close.

"Stay with me, Nikki," Casey told her. "Close your eyes and block out everything but your breathing."

Nikki followed his instructions. She didn't want to be the one to put the people she loved at risk. She wouldn't be putting just RJ in danger, but Brandon and Justin, too.

It took too long, but after a while she was able to push her animal under and felt steadier.

"Good job," Casey praised. "Now look."

Dylan had somehow figured out how to get the tiger off him and was taking quick bites before backing up. The tiger was starting to tire and wasn't moving out of the way fast enough.

Samson was knocked from going after Justin, flying through the air. RJ followed, growling and stalking. RJ was just magnificent. He was almost the size of Dylan, but the muscles in his chest and shoulders were bigger.

Inside, her own wolf started to calm as she watched him, noting he was okay and that her family was still safe.

"It's almost over," Casey said, loosening his hold.

She had forgotten he still had a grip on her.

Inside the circle, the wolf finally managed to pin the tiger with his jaws locked onto the feline's jugular. Dylan shook his head, biting down, and the tiger fought even harder.

"If you wish to submit, start to shift," Prince Zachary stated, his voice no-nonsense. "Or Dylan can end your life."

A collective gasp traveled through the Pack as the tiger transformed back to man. Dylan released his hold and backed away a few steps but stayed in wolf form. It was only a few seconds until Fred lay in the center of the circle, panting.

Oh, God, he's done it. Dylan's won.

"The challenge is over," Prince Zachary declared. "Dylan Cross is the winner and new Alpha of the Pack."

A cheer rose from the Pack, drowning out the howl of one lone wolf. Nikki turned in time to see Samson coming at her while RJ's back was turned as he looked toward his brother. Her wolf had had enough. She ripped out of Casey's hold and finally let her animal take control. She only managed to get out of her pants before she was on all fours and changing. Samson knocked into her and she could hear RJ and the others start forward.

She snarled at them to stay away and faced her foe. She wasn't going to let anyone else get hurt. This was over. Dylan was the Alpha. Brandon, Justin and RJ had fought and bled for the Pack. Samson needed to know that he would never win against them.

Nikki launched herself at Samson just as the other wolf did the same toward her. They slammed together, but Nikki was smaller and quicker. She turned in the air to put him under her and as they hit the ground hard and rolled, she clamped down on his throat.

He lifted her off her feet and she was thrown back a long distance. Nikki landed with a thud but used the momentum to regain her footing. To the side, both Brandon and RJ were being held in place. Justin was yelling something, but she couldn't make out the words. Samson's teeth on her ankle pulled her from the crowd.

Nikki swiped her paw down his face, causing him to roar.

That was music to her ears.

Samson backed off and Nikki was relieved — she didn't know how long she could have kept up the fight. She lowered herself into a pouncing position in case this was another trick.

He leaped and she wasn't surprised. Only his death was going to end this.

Nikki used the power of her back legs to launch herself from the ground. The force with which she hit Samson knocked the breath from her chest. She landed in a heap with him, only just remembering to protect herself. Samson snarled, but she had a better hold. Nikki latched on to his neck with her fangs.

He kicked at her, the claws of his legs digging into her stomach, but she wasn't letting go. The sting only enraged her further. She bit down until blood started to flow. Samson went limp in her hold and whimpered. The son of a bitch was great at starting fights, but it didn't seem to her that he could end them very well.

"Nikki." Dylan kneeled down next to her. "He submits to

you. You need to release him."

She shook her head, tearing more of his throat. Didn't Dylan understand that all of this was Samson's fault? If she let him go, then he'd attack RJ or her brother again. He wasn't going to accept Dylan as his Alpha. Nikki's wolf was done being the protected one. She was young and strong and could make sure no harm came to those she cared about.

"He will be taken care of," Dylan assured her. He placed his hand on her head. "Let him go now."

The power of her Alpha flowed through her. Nikki resisted, though. She didn't want to release Samson. This entire mess was his fault.

"Nikki."

RJ's voice sounded desperate. Was he hurt? She released her hold on Samson and dropped him to the ground. Spinning she searched for RJ. He was crouched, wearing a torn pair of jeans. She limped her way over and he opened his arms.

Nikki nuzzled his bare chest before licking away the sweat and blood. He was unhurt — that was enough to calm her racing heart. His scent was one of concern for her and no longer full of fear.

"It's okay," he said. "It's all over."

She whimpered, trying to get even closer. The adrenaline was ebbing and she began to shake. Damn, she was tired. Even the thought of transforming to her human shape seemed like too much effort.

"Is she okay?"

Nikki turned her head toward Brandon. It was hard to pull herself away from RJ, but she needed to make sure Brandon was okay. Unlike RJ, Brandon was fully dressed. She dug her nose into his stomach to see if he was hiding any injuries.

"I'm fine, pup," he said, ruffling her fur with his fingers.

It had been a long time since she'd been called a pup. Nikki had missed it. She play-growled knocking into his knees. He stumbled but didn't fall. It wasn't as though Nikki wanted to hurt him, but the animal side of her could use some Pack time. Well, some time that didn't involve a challenge, fighting and blood. She pawed at his thigh.

"Behave," Brandon ordered, but he was smiling.

"Can you shift?" RJ asked, pulling her into his arms.

She lowered herself to sit on his lap. All around them, the shifters who'd transformed were dressing and talking. Nikki didn't see any felines or Samson any longer. She tensed, not liking that no one was on guard.

"We've already got them out of here. My team is helping to get them secured and to the sheriff's department. We're safe," RJ soothed.

Nikki searched the faces of those around her. Brandon, Dylan, Justin, Ben, Casey and the Prince all were watching her. *Okay, it's over.* She laid her head against RJ's arm. She was tired.

"Can you shift?" RJ repeated his question.

Nikki closed her eyes and pictured her human form. When nothing happened, she whined looking at RJ.

"The wolf just needs to be in charge for a little while," Casey said. "She held off shifting as long as she could, but when Samson attacked her the wolf broke free." He petted her. "Nothing to worry about."

Nikki was scared. This had never happened to her. She was stuck in her wolf form! Panic filled her as she desperately tried to force the transformation.

"Hey!" RJ grasped her snout. "Stay calm. There's been times after a battle it's taken me a while to transform. The more relaxed you are, the faster everything will return to normal."

This can't be happening. Once the challenge was over it should be time to celebrate.

"Let's get everyone over to the house," Dylan suggested. "The rest of the Pack has left."

"The Alpha house," RJ stated. "We're going to the Alpha house." There was a short round of applause before RJ stood with her in his arms. Nikki licked at his face. She didn't need to be carried. She had four paws that worked just fine.

"Stop," he said with a laugh. "Just let me hold you. It scared the shit out of me when I saw you take on Samson."

Just like it had with her.

Nikki laid her chin on his shoulder as he strolled toward the vehicles. So much had happened in the last few hours. There was no place that she'd rather be than in RJ's arms.

Chapter Eight

RJ relaxed into the couch with Nikki cuddled into his side after quick showers for everyone. Across the room, Zachary, Casey, Craig and Mike were settled on the floor. Dylan and Brandon took up the large chairs while Justin and Ben leaned against the couch beside him. Beers had been passed around and while the atmosphere was somber, RJ couldn't help the smile on his face.

Once he'd gotten Nikki back to his house, she'd been able to shift and they'd showered together. They'd had to make it quick, but he'd have more time with her later. He was excited to see her interaction with his former team.

Nikki and Casey were already teasing each other. RJ was pleased. He'd had a feeling she'd get along with the guys. It was important since he was already more than halfway in love with her. Nikki was everything he'd always wanted in a partner. Soon it would be time to put his cards on the table and ask her to stay with him.

"So what now?" Ben questioned. He was leaning against Justin's shoulder. Justin was trying not to be obvious, but RJ could see how he'd wrapped his arm around Ben's lower back.

"Now to protect the Pack," Dylan stated. "Cameron's already suggested that anyone who backed the felines or attacked during the challenge should leave the Pack. We might lose some of our members."

"It's for the best," Brandon said. Nikki's brother appeared more worn than the rest of them. RJ would have been worried about injuries, but Dylan had assured him that Brandon was okay. "Bringing unknown felines into the

Pack to challenge…" He shook his head. "We're so fucking lucky no one was killed."

"It's not your fault, Brandon," Nikki spoke up.

He shrugged. "I should have done more. I never expected Samson to have become so lost."

It was Zachary who sat forward to address Brandon. "You couldn't have known. When it mattered, you stepped up to protect your family and Pack. I saw you throw yourself into several situations during the challenge to protect many in this room. That's what matters."

Brandon sighed. "Thanks." He didn't look convinced, but RJ figured it would take time for the events of the evening to be dealt with.

"You're going to have to recover quickly," Zachary went on to say.

RJ snapped his head up to stare at the Prince. "What's going on?"

Zachary peered around the room then his gaze settled on Dylan. "Cameron's updated you on the plans to go public."

"Yes." Dylan gave a slow nod. "He said the Council will let us know."

"Well." Zachary wrapped his arm around his mate's shoulder. Casey gripped his thigh. That didn't seem good. "I got the call on the way here. Two weeks."

"*Two weeks?*" Nikki repeated in shock. RJ knew just how she felt. He'd known it was in the plans, but RJ figured there'd be still months or even years to go.

"The Council is ready," Zachary said. "The announcement will be given in a speech with the President of the US. The Council will have several shifters there at the time."

"You'll be there," RJ guessed. It would make sense to have the most powerful feline, the Prince of his species, along with the wolf shifters.

"I have agreed to stand with them," Zachary stated.

Casey was frowning and Craig looked about ready to hop up. RJ knew these men better than he did his own brothers. They were worried.

"Do you need me?" RJ asked. He didn't want to leave his brother right when they were dealing with a new Pack, but he wouldn't turn his back on his unit.

"Not right now," Casey answered. He'd been RJ's commanding officer for the last ten years and RJ trusted that Casey would call him if he was needed. After Zachary had been kidnapped several months ago, Casey wouldn't take a chance with Zach's safety. "We might tag you for the actual day, but right now stay here and make sure your brother and Pack are safe. We don't know what is going to happen after the announcement is made."

"But you expect trouble?" Nikki asked. She leaned forward and RJ grunted. He wanted to keep holding her. He'd still not recovered from seeing Samson attacking her.

"Yes," Zachary and Casey answered together.

"Damn," RJ muttered. The dust hadn't settled quite yet and already the next issue was arising. He had to wonder if his life was ever going to be easy. After years of service for his country, all he wanted was to be able to take some time to settle in and enjoy being retired. Instead he'd had to deal with the threat of a challenge to his brother and now the unknown danger of the shifters going public.

Nikki slid her hand over his knee, making him aware of something else he'd wanted to take care of. RJ was certain she'd be a part of his future, though his life was here and she didn't even live in town. They needed to have a serious talk.

"It's not going to be easy," Zachary said. "However, I fully support this move. We need better protection."

"At least our town is full of shifters and those who know about us," Dylan said. "If any strangers show up, we'll be able to easily spot them."

"I'll prepare a new schedule for the deputies," Brandon added. "Once we have the exact date, we'll run double shifts until we know how the public is reacting."

"That's a good idea." Dylan nodded in approval. RJ was surprised to see the two of them working so well together.

Sure, Dylan had asked Brandon to be his Beta due to Cameron's recommendation, but RJ had thought it would take more time for the bond to form between Alpha and Beta.

"I'll stick around for a little bit as well, unless you need me with you?" Mike said to Casey.

No, stay here," Casey said. "We'll touch base before the announcement is made."

Nikki yawned snuggling to his side.

"For now, let's work out where everyone is going to sleep," RJ said. "It's been a long night."

"If Nikki is staying here, someone can take her room," Brandon offered.

"Yeah." She didn't even lift her head from RJ's chest.

"Zachary and Casey can have her room. I'll sleep on the couch in case of trouble," Craig stated, standing.

"I've got this place covered," Mike said.

RJ didn't think anyone needed to be on guard, but that didn't mean he wasn't relieved to know his best friend would keep an eye out. "You ready for bed?" he asked Nikki.

She rolled her head to peer up at him and grinned.

Immediately, he responded to the heat in her gaze. *Oh, the evening is just getting started.* RJ pushed himself off the couch before leaning down to pull her after him. Brandon stepped up and RJ moved away for Brandon to embrace Nikki.

"You scared the shit out of me tonight. Don't think we won't be discussing that later," he whispered to her.

RJ grinned. He had a few things to say about that as well.

"I know." She nodded.

Justin was the next in line for hugs so RJ crossed the room to his team.

"I can't thank you enough for being here," he said to Zachary. "I don't know what we would have done."

"It was my pleasure to be able to assist you after everything you'd done for me," Zachary responded.

RJ was proud he'd been able to rescue Zachary when the man had been taken by his cousin. The months-long search had been hard, but he'd met a couple of great people along the way and RJ could look at the entire mission as a success.

"When you need us, you call," Casey demanded, yanking RJ into a hug. "I'll kick your ass if you don't."

"Yes, sir." He pounded on Casey's back. "I promise."

Next, he shook hands with Craig, who wasn't much of a touchy-feely guy. Craig nodded toward Nikki. "You have someone real special there."

RJ followed his gaze. "I know." He did.

"We'll see you for breakfast in the morning," Casey ordered. "I heard the diner makes some fantastic pancakes."

"Sure," RJ agreed.

"Bring your girl. I want to get to know her better."

RJ waited until their guests were gone and Dylan and Ben were headed to bed. He turned to Mike. "I can't thank you enough for calling the team. It didn't even dawn on me to do so."

Mike shrugged. "I'm just glad they made it here on time. I didn't think we'd be fighting felines, but I thought Zachary's position would help. Show Samson that we had some major power behind us."

"I'm just glad it's all over," RJ said.

"Me, too," Mike agreed. "Now on to the next the stage of our civilian life."

"Yeah. And I thought retirement was going to be boring."

Mike chuckled; slapping him on the back. "You better get your woman to bed. It looks like she's going to fall asleep on her feet."

RJ turned around to see Nikki trying to hide a yawn behind her hand. "Come on," he said.

Nikki slid easily under his arm while they walked down the hall. She'd been through a lot that night and even if he just got to hold her, that would be enough.

"Let's get you tucked in bed," RJ said.

Nikki laughed. "I think we can do better than that."

"I don't want to wear you out. You did fight another shifter tonight. One who was much bigger than you."

"I'd rather you made love to me until I can't think straight. I don't want to dream."

He liked the way she thought. If Nikki needed him to stop her from replaying the fight, then RJ was not going to let her down. He opened his bedroom door in a second and pushed her inside. She laughed and, walking backward, started to lift her shirt over her head.

"First one naked gets to be on top," she teased.

He didn't care who was on top as long as he got her naked. So he pounced and helped her undress. They fumbled a little when her jeans caught on the shoes she still hadn't removed. They laughed and tugged them off together until she was finally undressed.

"Now you," she murmured and reached for his belt buckle.

"In a minute," he told her and eased her onto the mattress. He fell on top of her and started to kiss her once again. He mapped her body with his hands, learning where she was sensitive and how much pressure she liked. She was soft in all the right places.

Nikki arched into him, dragging her nails down his back. He shuddered with arousal. He liked the thought of her marks on his body. "RJ...please. Don't tease."

He just chuckled and continued his assault, feeding on her ripe breasts, which were full and begging for attention. She liked the way he flicked her nipples with his tongue, if the volume of her moans was any indication. RJ trailed his mouth down as he slipped his fingers inside. Her pussy, already wet and swollen, called to him. He buried his face in her sex and breathed deep. Her scent beckoned to every part of him. Man and wolf both wanted to claim her. To mark her where no other person would ever lay a hand on her again. It was way too soon to even consider making that type of commitment, but that didn't mean RJ didn't feel the need.

He licked at her, slowly at first, but as she spread wider for him, he feasted, nibbling until her shouts of ecstasy bounced off the walls. When she climaxed against his mouth, he sucked down her sweet essence. But it wasn't enough. He pulled away from her and flipped her over. She landed on her knees. Nikki opened her legs and lowered her shoulders to the pillow. RJ held her down with a hand on the back of her neck while he released his raging hard-on with the other.

His wolf howled at the show of dominance and submission.

And she arched, moaning and begging for him to take her.

So much — so much emotion, so much passion. There was no doubt that the woman under him was meant to be his future. He slid inside her little by little, drawing out both her pleasure and his.

Her body welcomed him.

He withdrew, nice and slow, then slammed inside.

"Yes…yes," she urged him on, still drunk on passion.

RJ growled and let himself go, pounding into her, lifting her hips and claiming her body like he wanted to do to her soul. Nikki met him thrust for thrust. The slaps of flesh coming together and their cries of joy filled the room. His orgasm came in a rush. She yelled, clamping her inner muscles around his cock, and pushed him hard over the edge.

He collapsed above her, panting in her ear until she started to giggle. He rose enough to brush her sweaty hair out of her face. She grinned up at him.

"Just keeps getting better and better," she said, her voice husky and pleased.

RJ laughed, pulled out of her gently and fell back down, at her side. "We have breakfast tomorrow with the guys, so we really do need to get some sleep."

When Nikki didn't respond, her turned his head and found her asleep, her breathing soft. Well, shit, he was going to have to move them up the mattress and under the covers.

With a sigh, he rolled off the bed. He peered down at her. Nikki was just as beautiful sound asleep as she was with passion in her eyes. RJ had no idea how he'd gotten so lucky as to have caught her attention. But he was going to have to figure out a way to keep it.

She barely even responded when he yanked down a corner of the bedspread and lifted her into the spot. A snuffle, a moan and she was snuggling down. With a shake of his head, he headed to the bathroom to clean up so he could join her.

RJ could get used to having Nikki in his life and bed, just like this. *All too easily…*

* * * *

RJ locked the door to his shop before sliding onto his bike and heading home. He waved at Brandon as he passed the sheriff's office. Brandon lifted his hand, smiling as he did so.

Their relationship had done a complete one-eighty in the past two weeks. Now that they had to work together every day making sure the Pack was ready for the big announcement, they'd found a common ground. That and Nikki had threatened to rip off their balls if they didn't start acting like adults.

His woman was scary sometimes.

RJ smiled. *My woman.* RJ thought of her that way, but, as busy as everyone still was, they hadn't had the talk about the future yet.

The short drive to the house where everyone was meeting was enjoyable. It was cooling down and he needed his thick leather jacket when he was on his bike. Nikki had expressed interest in joining him for a long ride, but there hadn't been time. After he closed the shop at night, his usual routine was to report to Dylan and the rest of the inner circle so plans could be made for the future on how to handle any danger to the Pack.

Luckily he was able to crawl into bed with her every night. Either his or hers, but RJ always found himself with Nikki in his arms when he did turn in. She appeared to be just as smitten with him as he was with her.

It wouldn't be tonight, though.

All their preparations would come down to how the public handled what was being released tonight. The shifters knew what was going to be said. The other millions of people in the world had no idea how their lives would change.

He pulled under the carport and saw that everyone but Brandon had arrived.

Even from the yard, the laughing and joking could be heard clearly though the open door. RJ stomped up the wood steps and entered. He was glad that Casey hadn't needed him or Mike. There was a good chance that his little town would be just fine and wouldn't get hit hard by violence, but RJ still wanted to be there.

"Hey," Nikki greeted as she passed. She leaned close to bestow a quick kiss on him on her way to the kitchen.

Ben and Justin were settled in one of the big chairs while Mike, Max and a couple of the other inner circle Pack sprawled out on the floor.

Snacks and drinks were scattered around the room, probably thanks to Ben. Ben had always acted a bit of a mother hen, but now that Dylan was Alpha, he always had some fresh-cooked food available for when someone stopped by.

It wouldn't be long until Dylan moved into the Alpha house now that Cameron had left town. The house needed a little work and Dylan had a plan to make it his own while still allowing the place to remain comfortable to the Pack. RJ hadn't decided if he was going to join Dylan or not. A lot of his choice would come down to whether or not Nikki stayed in town.

RJ settled on the couch in front of the flat-screen television and accepted a bottle of beer from Nikki. She held her own bottle and relaxed next to him. Dylan entered the room at the same time as Brandon strolled in.

"You ready for this?" Brandon asked, sitting beside Nikki.

RJ glanced at his brother. Dylan hadn't said much about the upcoming announcement since he'd become Alpha. Even though Dylan would keep his word and go public with the rest of the world, no one was excited about the prospect of trouble.

"Hell, no," Dylan muttered before he began to pace.

"It's time," Ben said, picking up the remote and turning on the television. He raised the news up loud so they wouldn't miss a word.

At exactly seven o'clock, the picture on the screen switched to the private room full of reporters.

"Ladies and gentlemen...the President of the United States of America."

The leader of their country stepped up to the podium.

Nikki gripped RJ's hand and they exchanged worried glances. This wasn't the only place where the shifters' existence was being revealed to the public. There would be similar announcements made in other countries, until it was finally known around the world that some of the mystical creatures in movies and books were very real.

The shifters were now out in the open.

RJ had to give the Commander in Chief President Lawson credit. He spoke with intelligence and calmness as he informed the public about the existence of shifter-kind. The reporters in the room began screaming out questions, but President Lawson remained in control and simply held up a hand.

"I know you have questions," President Lawson stated. "Luckily, standing here with me are some people who have more knowledge about the situation and have agreed to come forward."

A tall, good-looking man with dark hair and a bright

smiled stepped up to the podium. "Hello ladies and gentlemen. My name is Tony."

"I wouldn't want to be that guy," Nikki whispered to RJ while shuddering.

RJ agreed as the wolf shifter continued to introduce himself and state facts about what he was. The man would probably end up with the biggest target on his back. No matter how much RJ hoped for the best outcome, in his gut he feared the worst. He had a feeling that the next couple of weeks and months would see the lives of those of his kind undergo a drastic change. He couldn't see how there wouldn't be panic.

"They've done a lot of work in preparation for this," Dylan said over the television.

"I hope so," RJ responded. He had to remain positive for his brother. Even though Dylan would pick up his unease over the situation, RJ didn't want to make things harder for Dylan.

"Shh," Ben hushed.

"You cannot be turned into a shifter," the man on the television was saying. "A scratch or bite is just urban myth. At no time and under no circumstance can you ever be changed into a shifter. You've been living side by side with us for centuries. Nothing is different now that you are aware of our existence."

"Do you think people are going to believe that?" Justin asked.

"Some will," Brandon replied. "Others will take time."

"What do we do in the meantime?" Justin questioned.

"We're lucky," Dylan stated. "If a stranger enters our town, we'll know about it. I'm going to open our Pack to others who need sanctuary from the human world."

"Wouldn't that make more sense if we weren't going public?" Ben asked.

"If the shifter had already been outed to the public, he can't join a Pack that's staying hidden without putting them at risk. If that shifter comes here, we can look out for them," Dylan explained.

"There's already been offers from the Council to my department for help within the sheriff's office. If we do start to take in shifters, they have men who can come help," Brandon informed them.

RJ hadn't realized how much their town was in danger of changing.

"The bigger cities are going to be the worst," Dylan said.

"It's a good thing you're not returning right away," Brandon said to Nikki. "I'd be worried sick."

Wait, what? RJ turned toward Nikki. "You're not?"

"Uh..." She glanced from her brother and back to him.

Brandon set his beer down. "I thought you said you were staying. I don't want you to be gone until we know how the humans are going to react."

"Why didn't you tell me?" RJ spoke over Brandon. He'd been worried sick and trying to figure out a way to talk to her and she was making the decision without him.

Nikki huffed then stood. "I also told you not to say anything yet," she said to Brandon.

"Oh yeah." Brandon said.

"Come here." She reached down and tugged him to his feet.

RJ followed as she led him out of the living room onto the front porch. Someone, probably Ben, had added several additional pieces of brown wicker furniture and some plants. With solar lights boarding the rails, the ambiance was almost romantic.

"I was going to talk to you," Nikki finally said when she stopped walking. She turned and looked up at him.

"Okay?" He was confused why they needed to have this conversation outside, though.

"I'm staying in town, although I'll still be taking assignments all over."

He frowned. That didn't sound good. Sure, RJ knew she had to work, but he didn't see why she couldn't do it from home.

"Why are you frowning?"

"You can't work from here?"

Nikki smiled. "I travel quite a lot to get the photographs for my articles. I usually finish everything up from my home base, which is going to be here."

Maybe I can go with her? If she was going to be out in the open, she needed someone to watch her back. RJ would have some trouble getting away while they were preparing for the future, but Nikki was important to him.

Nikki gave a deep sigh pulling away. She stalked over to the railing and leaned against it. "It's fine," she said. "I don't expect anything from you."

"What? Why not?"

"Hey, I was going to talk to you. Just because I'm staying in town doesn't mean that you have to make a commitment to me. I understand that you started this *thing* with me thinking I would be leaving."

"What in the hell are you talking about?" RJ said with a growl. Was Nikki actually trying to break up with him? *Oh, hell, no!* "You actually think you're going to live here and see other people?"

"RJ—"

"No," he stated. "I didn't start this *thing* with you thinking you would leave. I've been trying to think of a way to talk to you about our future, but every time I want to approach the topic, something happens. One way or another, we're going to make this *relationship* work."

"*Relationship?* You want to have a relationship with me?"

"Of course I do!" He threw up his hands in frustration.

"Then why are we fighting?" she yelled.

RJ started to laugh. Well, shit, they were arguing. He almost fell over as he couldn't contain his amusement. When he finally got hold of himself, he flopped into one of the chairs and motioned to Nikki. "Come here," he said, breathless.

She had a bewildered expression on her face, but luckily for him she strolled over and dropped into his lap. "You done laughing?"

"It just struck me as funny. We were both too worried about what was going to happen we didn't talk to each other," RJ said.

"Yes. I'm aware of that. However, I don't find it as amusing as you did. And why the hell were you making faces when I said I was staying? It's your fault I thought you didn't want me to stay."

"I want you to stay," he assured her. "I just don't like the idea of you traveling when all of this is going on."

"Now you sound like Brandon."

"I always thought he was a smart man," RJ quipped.

"Liar. You couldn't stand him. You just like when he is as over-protective as you are."

He shrugged. It wasn't as though he could dispute her words. "Fine, but he's right."

"Which makes you right," Nikki pointed out.

"There is that. I just don't think you should be going off to places you don't know when we aren't sure where the threats, if any, will come from."

"I'll be careful," she said. "I do know how to do my job."

"I've seen your work online, remember. You're very good. I just hate the idea of you traveling alone."

Her smile lit up her entire face. "I'd forgotten you researched me."

"Don't think I've forgotten you got classified information as well. We are going to discuss that one day."

"But not today?" she asked, running her hands up his chest.

"No, right now we're going to figure out living arrangements."

"I have my room at my house," she said.

"That's fine as long as I'm welcome to stay there with you. Or you could stay here. But I don't want to sleep apart from you."

"You don't...you don't think it's too soon?" she questioned.

"I really don't care," he replied with complete honesty. "As long as I get to hold you every night and wake with you in the morning. Especially if you plan to go out of town a lot."

"Not a lot, but it will happen. But when I'm in town I'd love to be with you every chance I can."

"There's an apartment above my shop," he informed her. "I haven't done anything with it yet, but maybe it's time I did."

"Oh, really?" She practically purred the words.

"A bedroom suite and maybe even an office area. That way if I'm downstairs working, you would still be close by."

Nikki leaned forward and nuzzled him. "I like the sound of that. I still want to watch you work someday."

"And have you thought about a tattoo?"

"Maybe," she teased. "If I had the right artist."

RJ cupped her face. "Like I would let anyone else put their hands on you."

"What about your hands?" she asked, rubbing her leg against his.

He ran his hands down her neck to cup her breasts. "I'm pretty sure you could talk me into anything."

"Hmm..." Nikki leaned in to kiss him and RJ allowed himself to just relax and let her control the speed.

At least they were on the same page in regard to their relationship. And it was a relationship, damn it. Nikki was his and he wasn't about to let her go without one hell of a fight.

Chapter Nine

Nikki wasn't surprised when one of the papers she'd worked for in the past called her early in the morning just days after the announcement about shifters had come. Every news channel in the nation was following the events that were unfolding.

Just as everyone had worried, there were groups of humans who had banded together in order to protect themselves from the 'unholy creatures'. That was what her kind was being called — unholy. *As though God or whatever deity they use would want the capture and murder of innocent people.*

"Craig, I'm sure that man is very busy. He just came out to the entire world as a shifter," Nikki said to the editor-in-chief she'd worked with several other times. She didn't understand how Craig thought she'd be able to get an interview with Tony. And on top of that, Craig actually wanted her to photograph him in his 'other' form.

"Come on, Nikki!" Craig demanded. "You've always been able to get people to talk to you. It's the reason we call on you for the tough assignments."

Nikki had decided what to do about her own shifter status. Eventually where she lived would be revealed and her secret would be out. But writing an article would be one-sided. She couldn't be objective. "I don't think I'm the right person for this job."

"I know you probably don't want to be around one of those...creatures, but we need this. I'll even send one of the guys to act as your security if you're worried about your safety. We don't know how these animals will react, after all."

Oh, shit, Craig's one of the asshole humans. It took all Nikki's control not to snarl into the phone. "I don't need protection," she managed.

"Still, I would feel better if you took one of the other guys. I want to a full series showing how dangerous these things really are. Can you believe some people just want to live next to these monsters? It's our duty to show the world the truth."

Nikki mentally counted to ten. If she allowed the words that wanted to escape her mouth out, she'd never work for that paper again. Too bad they'd always paid her well. It wasn't as though she needed the money. Living at home and having her savings account meant she could stay comfortable for years, but Nikki liked her profession. Craig wasn't the nicest guy in the world, but he'd always treated her fairly. "I'm sorry, but—"

"Don't say no!" Craig cut her off.

She glanced up when the door opened allowing Brandon to stroll in with RJ at his heels. They'd gone on a run in their wolf forms to patrol the boundary of town before she'd woken up.

"Hey, you're awake," RJ sauntered close enough to give her a kiss. He paused in the middle of leaning down. "What's wrong?"

Nikki shook her head.

"Are you listening to me?" Craig yelled into the phone.

She sighed, more so when RJ narrowed his eyes at her cell. "Yes, Craig, I heard every word you said. I'm sorry, I don't need time to think about it. I can't take this assignment." She ended the call. He could argue with her or she said something she'd regret.

"Who was that?" RJ demanded.

"One of the editors I've worked with," she said. Nikki dropped her head into her hands. In the last several years, she'd never turned down a job if she wasn't already on assignment. It didn't feel right to allow someone else to do what Craig wanted, but Nikki just couldn't do what he'd asked.

"What did he say?" Brandon asked. He wasn't growling, but she still picked up the anger in his tone.

Nikki stood and refilled her coffee as she relayed the conversation to Brandon and RJ. By the time she had finished, RJ was fuming.

"It's not a bad idea," Brandon commented.

"What?" RJ snapped.

"Excuse me?" Nikki spat.

Brandon waved his hand. "Not what your boss wanted, but doing a series about what it's like being a shifter."

"You want her to expose herself?" RJ shouted. "Hell, no!"

"She doesn't have to write about herself," Brandon stated. "Dylan could talk to the Council to see if they know someone who wouldn't mind being the subject of the article. That way, Nikki could work with them and whatever shifter volunteers."

"That isn't actually what this asshole asked for," RJ pointed out.

"I'm still in the room," Nikki announced before the two men decided every detail about her life.

"Sorry." RJ ducked his head.

Brandon crossed his arms over his chest. "It's a good idea."

It was. Nikki could agree with that, but did she really want to take on something this big? Shit, of course she did. She'd spent her entire life searching for a story that would make her career. And if it benefited the shifters, who would it hurt? "I'll think about it."

Brandon grinned. "I'm going to give Dylan a heads-up about this guy, though. If he can call the Council to warn them, maybe they'll be able to keep Tony from doing any interviews that might put us in a bad light."

She nodded. Her brother left the room so she turned her attention to RJ. He sat brooding at the table. "What?"

"I don't like it."

"Like Brandon said, I don't have to be writing about myself."

"But if you're seen siding with shifters, you could be out in danger."

"Have you forgotten that I am a shifter?" she asked. Really, the protectiveness was hot, but she could take care of herself as well. "Eventually someone is going to figure out I live with a Pack."

He grunted.

"Plus it could really help," she said. "Right now, we only have the one big announcement. If people are going to be writing about us anyway, we should at least make sure that they get their facts right."

"I'm waiting for you to start spouting off constitutional rights and all that."

Nikki laughed. RJ knew her too well already. "Well..."

He held up a hand. "I know." With a heavy sigh, RJ leaned back in his chair. "There's already been a riot in Chicago, illegal hunting has risen around the country and people have gotten hurt. I can't stop myself from worrying about you."

"I don't want you to," she told him. "I like the fact that you care about me so much. This is something that I want — no, need — to do."

"Fine, but I want to know every detail and if you leave our territory, you take someone with you," he demanded.

"I have no problem keeping you informed, but I'm a big girl. I don't need a travel buddy."

"You don't know what you need yet. That's why it's better to be safe than sorry. If you get into trouble, you'll have someone you know there to watch your back," RJ argued.

"Who?" Nikki asked. "You and Brandon have to be here to help Dylan and make sure our Pack is safe. Justin and Ben have jobs."

"I'll ask Mike." RJ brightened as he spoke. "He's been looking for something to do and this is perfect. He is a highly decorated military man and he won't let anyone hurt you."

As much as she wanted to argue with RJ, he was making sense. "We'll see." Shit, she might not be committing to anything at the moment, but they both knew she would.

"It'll all get worked out," Brandon stated, walking in. "Dylan and Mike are on their way."

"I didn't say yes," she pointed out.

Brandon snorted. "I know how your mind works, little sister. You've probably already outlined the first story."

The first two, but I won't be admitting it. "You need to butt out, Brandon. Just because I moved back here doesn't mean that you get to run my life. I'm a grown woman."

He surprised her by sitting in the chair beside hers and taking her hand. "I'm not trying to manage your life."

Nikki raised an eyebrow.

"No, really. You've been gone a while and I'm so fucking glad you've come home. I guess I'm just worried you won't find enough excitement to keep you here," Brandon said.

"Gee, thanks," RJ muttered.

"Nothing against you, man," Brandon said to RJ. "But it's one of the things that keeps me up at night."

"I told you that you didn't have to worry. I want to be here," she assured her brother. Nikki had never regretted her decision to leave, but she hated that Brandon saw it as a negative.

"It's my issue and I'm trying to get over it," Brandon said. "It helps that you seem happier now than I've ever seen you."

She glanced at RJ. That statement had the definite ring of truth.

"I don't just mean lover boy here," Brandon said. "You've reconnected with your friends, you've become a role model to the teenagers and we have family night again. I don't want to lose you."

"You're not going to," she promised. Sure, she didn't know what the future held, but Nikki wouldn't repeat the mistakes she'd made in the past. She could have gone to school and started working and still come to visit. There was no reason for her to have cut herself off from her family.

"I'm going to hold you to that," Brandon said hugging her.

She returned the embrace, holding him as tight as she could. When they pulled away, RJ had risen from the table and started making a pot of coffee.

"I'm going to shower before the guys get here," Brandon said. "I have to get to the station."

"Sure." She got to her feet.

She walked up behind RJ and wrapped her arms around his waist to rest her forehead between his shoulder blades. "Thanks."

"I'm glad you have him and Justin," RJ said, his voice quiet. "I missed so much with my brothers and I regret that."

It seemed as though they both had some things to make up for with their families. "I see how Ben looks at you. You're his hero."

RJ just shrugged.

"It's true," she said. "And Dylan trusts you. That says a lot."

"I'm glad we came here." He turned and tugged her close to his chest.

Nikki loved the way they fit together. "Me, too."

When he kissed her, Nikki had to hand it to him. RJ never did anything by halves. Whatever act he was involved in, he gave his all. One kiss turned into two then three, until she was panting against his mouth.

Aroused and flushed, she stepped back. "That's not nice. Your brother is going to be here soon."

"His brother has arrived and is just waiting for the two of you to stop playing kissy face."

RJ groaned as Dylan strolled in from the living room.

"It's a good thing Justin let me in." Dylan made his way to the coffee pot. "I haven't had my coffee yet."

"Yes, Alpha," RJ responded. "I was just making it, Your

Majesty."

"Watch it or I'll put you on midnight duty for the next month and you'll have no time for sucking face."

"That's just mean." RJ pouted.

"I'll show you mean," Dylan said, pouncing on RJ.

RJ yelled; slipping from Dylan's grasp and pulling Nikki in front of him.

"Hey!" She threw up her arms.

"Save me!" RJ begged. "The mean Alpha is out to get me."

Dylan growled; trying to take a swipe at RJ around Nikki. RJ jumped away, shoving Nikki at his brother at the same time.

"Seriously, RJ?" she asked, laughing.

"Yeah, seriously, RJ?" Dylan mocked. "Hiding behind your girlfriend?"

"I'm not hiding," RJ defended. "I just can't kick your ass anymore because now you're my Alpha!"

"Like you could ever," Dylan taunted.

"You're all a bunch of children," Brandon declared, returning from his shower.

Nikki completely lost it when both RJ and Dylan turned to her older brother and stuck out their tongues. It was so not becoming of two alpha males. Brandon just shook his head, bitching while Nikki leaned against the counter laughing so hard she had tears in her eyes.

That of course gave Dylan the chance to jump on RJ and wrestle him to the floor.

They were still rolling around when Mike and Justin joined them. The way that Mike simply stepped over the two men told her this wasn't the first time he'd walked in on the brothers rough-housing.

Nor was he very worried about it.

Nikki wanted to learn more about his friends and the unit they'd made up. She knew better than to do it from research now, though. It would take time, but she wanted the stories to come from RJ, Mike and the others. A lot could get lost in reports and Nikki wanted to hear RJ's voice as he told her about his adventures.

It took about ten minutes, but RJ at last conceded to his brother and Dylan jumped to his feet to saunter to the table. Nikki stepped over to RJ and held out her hand. He grinned up at her with a wicked curve to his lips. That look did all kinds of things to make her stomach flutter.

If she wasn't careful, she would end up rolling around on the kitchen floor with him as well. Which wouldn't be good, since both their brothers were sitting at the table, watching.

"Are you finished?" she asked him.

"For now," RJ said, letting her help him to his feet. Not allowing her to get away from him, RJ had her against his hard body. "Although I wouldn't mind letting you take me down like that."

That sounded good to her. "Maybe later?"

"What are your plans this weekend?"

Nikki glanced from the guys gathered at the table then back at him. "Umm…"

"I want to take you somewhere."

"I don't know if I will have time."

"Think about it," RJ said. "Me, you, my bike, the mountains."

Yeah, Nikki wanted that. She hadn't ever been on a bike and she trusted RJ to keep her safe. Plus, if they were going to have a real chance at a relationship, they needed some time alone. Too many brothers, Pack members, and danger around every corner. *Don't the two of us deserve a little time and space together?*

"Just a few days," RJ pressed.

"I want to say yes," she admitted.

"So say yes."

What do I have to lose? While Dylan and the Council worked out the details of her plan, she could escape with RJ for some alone time. "Yes."

"If you two are done, I want to hear about this idea you have, Nikki," Dylan said. "From what Brandon told me about it, I'm one hundred percent in. I think the Council will be, too."

She shook her head but sat down so she could discuss her ideas with her Alpha and family. RJ stood behind her with his hand on the back of her chair. She liked how he always seemed to stay close to her, as if he was protecting her from the world, but still allowed her to speak her mind. "I think a series of photos showing that a shifter is both human and more is ideal."

"Photos?" Dylan asked.

"That's how I tell my stories. I might take a hundred pictures, but one will be perfect. It will show everything we need to without words. I'll write an article to go with it, but it's the photo that will draw people in. If we can just show the humans our humanity, I think it'll make a difference."

"I've seen her work," RJ said. "It is powerful."

"It is," Brandon agreed.

Pride filled her and Nikki had to look away from the others to regain her composure. It wasn't often that she'd felt such sincerity when it came to her passion. She knew Brandon cared about her, but to hear the words meant so very much.

"How will you get it published?" Dylan questioned.

"I'll shop around for the right place," Nikki informed him. "I've done it in the past."

"So what do you need?" Dylan asked. "How can I help?"

"We need the right shifter," Nikki said. "Someone who the humans will be able to relate to. They need to see us as something more than a threat, to know we're not just animals."

"The Council should help with that," Dylan said. "They know of every shifter in the world."

"Why can't one of us do it?" Brandon asked.

"I'd prefer it not be someone I have a connection with," Nikki stated. "It'll be better using a stranger. That way no one can say I gave a biased report. It'll be iffy enough when people learn I'm a shifter."

"Is this going to hurt your career?" Justin asked.

Nikki shrugged. "If my conversation this morning with one of the editors is any indicator, it could possibly."

"Damn." Justin shook his head.

Nikki wasn't upset any longer, though. Craig was an ass, but his opinion didn't matter in the end. She was finished trying to please people for the sake of her career. It was the people in the room, her friends in the Pack and the man she was falling in love with who held any real meaning. "It's okay. I might have to distance myself from a few people, but I'm gaining so much more."

RJ rested his hand on her shoulder. "There might even be more people willing to talk to you. Not all of the publicity has been negative."

"That's true," she agreed. "I've worked for papers and sites all over the world. It appears that the east side of the country has been a little more willing to accept us than the west."

"Then that's where we need to concentrate the most," Dylan said. "It helps that the Council compound is in California. They'll know that area well."

"I wonder if you'll get to go there?" Justin said. "Wouldn't that be awesome?"

"I don't know of anyone not involved with the Council who has seen their property."

"I met a couple of guys who work directly for them," RJ stated. "They're still part of their own Packs, but they work part-time for the Council. They were both pretty cool guys."

"Maybe the Council can send one of them," Nikki suggested.

RJ shrugged. "I suppose we could ask, if that's what you're looking for."

Nikki pressed her lips together. "It's really not. Here's what I was thinking."

* * * *

The rumble and vibration of the motorcycle under her

was both foreign and exciting at the same time. They'd had to move up the trip before the weekend since the Council's selection for the shifter she'd be interviewing was due by the week. The Council wanted Nikki to go ahead and get started.

Now that the Council was involved, Nikki's excitement over the project had grown into nerves. It wasn't as though the entire shifter population depended on her article, but Nikki was still feeling the pressure.

When RJ had shown up with his saddlebags packed and told her to climb on the back of his bike, she'd not hesitated. For a couple of hours, she could forget all about her plans and the upcoming weeks and just be free.

Several times, RJ turned his head to check on her, but Nikki was enjoying the two-hour drive into the mountains. She had her arms around RJ's slim waist, feeling each muscle strain. She couldn't wait until they arrived at the camping spot to get him naked and inside her.

The change from gravel to dirt had her tightening her hold on him.

For a first ride on the back of RJ's motorcycle, she hadn't done too bad. The cool night air felt great against her skin and, inside, her wolf was howling to get out. It seemed the animal part of her enjoyed the speed and adventure.

After another twenty minutes of winding roads, RJ pulled in to a secluded spot before he shut off the bike. She waited until he motioned her off then climbed from the motorcycle.

Luckily RJ was quick enough to catch her when her wobbly legs failed to hold her.

"Easy," he murmured against her cheek. "You have to take it slow."

"Wow, I wasn't expecting that," she admitted. Even her butt was sort of numb.

RJ chuckled. She had a feeling that he knew exactly what she was going through.

"You could have warned me," she accused.

"But then I wouldn't have been able to sweep in and

rescue you."

"Really?" Nikki said with a snort. *"Sweep?"*

RJ swung her up and into his arms in one easy movement. "See, sweep."

Okay, so that was quite impressive. She wrapped her arms around his neck and pulled him forward. "My hero," she murmured then kissed him.

He responded quickly and with passion. Their tongues dueled while she held him close. It hadn't been that long since they'd made love and she still needed him with a desperation that unnerved her.

"Hold that thought," he requested, breaking away. "We have to set up the tent before it gets too dark."

"But I like the dark," she replied, waggling her eyebrows at him.

"We have all night," he promised her. "We'll set up camp, go for a run in our wolf forms, come back and eat then I'll love on you all night long."

"That sounds good," she responded. "But I have a counter-offer."

"What's that?"

"We make love now, then set up the tent, go for that run, make love again, eat then you spend the rest of the night fucking my brains out," she said.

The increase in his heartbeat and obvious reaction belied his shake of his head. Oh, he wanted her. Nikki pushed her breasts against him.

"You little minx," he accused.

Nikki merely smiled in return.

Instead of laying her out, RJ set her on her feet and slapped her ass.

"Hey!" she complained.

"Help me unpack," he ordered. "Then we'll maybe alter my plan a bit."

"Fine." She stomped to the bike, but it was all for show. RJ had a pretty good idea. While she'd seen him in his wolf form, they hadn't had the time to shift and run together.

Actually, she hadn't transformed with anyone other than her brothers. The few times she'd managed on her own had been so different. A wolf, shifter or natural, was meant to be surrounded by Pack.

They unloaded the bike and RJ went about setting up the tent while Nikki checked out the area around them. She'd expected some sort of camp ground, but RJ had to have found the most unused spot in the area.

"Have you ever been here?" she asked him.

"Actually, Brandon told me about it."

"My brother?"

"I guess he used to come up here a lot when you and Justin were gone for the night," RJ said.

"Alone?" She didn't even want to think about the women her brother could have brought up here.

"I got the distinct impression that he was not alone."

"Eww!" She wanted to smack him.

"You asked," he responded, laughing.

"I didn't really want an answer, though."

"Why not?" RJ asked. "He's a man and, even though he was raising you and Justin, he had needs."

"Stop!" she ordered. "I do not need to think about my brother having sex."

RJ rose from where he'd finished setting up the tent then strolled over to her. "Oh, come on! He'd had to have brought women around."

"Sure he did," she admitted. "But it's not like they had sex in the kitchen during dinner. I don't want to talk about this. It's like discussing my dad's sex life."

He shook his head but dropped the subject. "So how about that run?"

"I'd like that. You're impressive as a wolf."

RJ pulled his shirt over his head. "This is the best part. Get naked."

"I see," she teased. "You just want me to strip for you."

"Of course I do." He winked. "Although I prefer to remove your clothes myself, but I think I'll have to refrain this time or we'll run out of light."

Eager, Nikki started to undress. She barely beat RJ but used the few minutes to admire him as he finished. The muscles in his arms, the wideness of his shoulders, and his erect cock. Damn, she really wanted to play with RJ. Well, in both human and furry forms they could have fun, but she didn't know which she wanted more.

"Stopping eying me like that," he stated, obviously amused.

"Are you sure you can shift like that?" She nodded to his hard-on.

"Yes," he replied with a grin. "First one who transforms gets to pick what we get to do after."

Nikki dropped down and closed her eyes, ignoring his warm chuckle. He might like torturing her, but if she changed first, she'd get her revenge. Picturing her wolf form, she concentrated on becoming her animal. The shift was natural and painless. One moment, she was kneeling as a human, then her body began to change. Fur sprouted first, then came contortions as her bones and body realigned.

Unlike depictions in Hollywood movies, becoming her wolf was so fast that it didn't hurt, which she was grateful for.

Once the change was complete, she shook herself hard, ruffling her fur. She glanced over to RJ, who sat watching her. Damn it, he'd beaten her.

Nikki dropped her chest to the ground and wagged her tail. He might have been able to shift faster than her, but that didn't mean she'd concede without a struggle. RJ rose before stalking toward her. As soon as he got close enough, she pounced on him.

Even though he moved fast, she still managed to nip at his hind leg then took off running.

She heard him close at her heels as she led him out of the camping spot and into the dense forest. The canopies above blocked out the remaining light and the temperature was much cooler. *Good thing I come with a fur coat.*

Changing direction when she caught the faint whiff of water, Nikki was only just able to avoid RJ knocking into her.

He growled, but she didn't even slow down.

This is fun.

It was always better to have company than to be alone enjoying nature. She'd forgotten that, over the years that she'd been away, and this was something else that RJ had given back to her.

The small creek came into view at the same time RJ leaped and sent her rolling. Nikki tucked in her chin and just went with the motion. Once she came to a stop, leaves and dirt covering her, she looked up at RJ. He stood over her, grinning. She beat her tail against the tree next to her, the *thump…thump…thump* echoing around them.

RJ leaned down and nosed her, but she batted his muzzle. She was just fine and hadn't been hurt.

In fact, she could even go for another chase.

Nikki stood. Instead of getting ready to take off once again, RJ nudged her toward the water. She padded along beside him until they both dipped their heads to drink.

The cold liquid was soothing as she drank. After getting her fill, she lifted her head to see that RJ had stepped away. Nikki began to turn but he lunged, knocking her into the creek.

She gave a loud howl of complaint. Okay, all good and fun, but the water was cold and she was going to get him back. RJ was on the bank, hopping around. *Oh, he thinks he's funny.*

Turning, Nikki began to use her tail to splash water at him.

Once he was soaked, she gazed at him, pleased. *Yep, not so smug now, is he?*

Nikki started toward dry land. RJ took several steps back before he ran at her and jumped right on top.

They both went under.

Using her back paws, she pushed away from him and

up to the surface. *What the hell?* They weren't felines and wolves didn't like water.

Instead of rushing out like she'd expected, RJ began to jump around, splashing her with water.

He's like a big kid.

Well, if RJ could let loose, so could she. Nikki pounced on him and they wrestled until she was panting with exhaustion. It couldn't have been more than fifteen minutes, but after the long run she was wiped out.

She pawed his face and whined.

RJ stopped trying to dunk her and nudged her toward the bank.

Nikki did one long shake to remove the excess water from her coat before plopping down. RJ lowered himself to curl around her. With night falling quickly, she closed her eyes as RJ's warmth seeped into her.

With his cuddling behind her, it didn't take long for Nikki to warm up and want to move on with the rest of their plans. She flipped over to face RJ and started to clean his muzzle. He nosed her neck, breathing in her scent while getting slowly to his feet. RJ began his transformation to human and she followed suit.

Once she was naked, lying on the bank of the creek, she shook her head. "Sometimes I forget you're supposed to be this big bad military guy."

With his hands on his hips, he grinned. "If there is one thing I learned by traveling around the world for someone else's wars, it's that you have to find your fun where you can."

"And that's pushing me into ice-cold water?"

"It wasn't that cold," he responded.

"I don't know." Nikki folded her hands behind her head. "I think you should come over her and warm me up."

RJ's reaction was immediate. His pupils dilated as he sauntered closer. He was already half hard and just the sight of his shaft had her mouth watering. "You see something you like?" he teased. RJ gripped his cock and stroked.

"You know I do."

"But we're supposed to go back to camp and eat," he said.

"I think it's my turn to decide on the activities."

"You didn't win the shifting contest."

Okay, he had her there. "Well, if you don't want me, I guess I'll have to take care of myself." She ran her palms down herself, cupping her breasts. Nikki arched as she pushed the soft mounds into her fingers.

RJ moaned and stroked himself faster. "Pluck your nipples."

She complied, feeling the tingle all over her body.

"Yeah," he praised. "Slide one land lower."

She'd never felt so dirty and sexy at the same time. Having him tell her how to touch herself was arousing. Nikki used her right hand to trail down her stomach to her wet, slick pussy. She was ready for him. Wanted RJ inside her. Although she could handle a little more playing.

"Tease your clit," he ordered.

The small little nub was already swollen as she circled and pressed down on it. Nikki couldn't hold in her groan of pleasure.

"So hot," he murmured.

"RJ…"

"Keep going," he told her. "Finger yourself."

Damn, she might climax just from his words. Already her breaths were coming out in pants, her breasts felt fuller and the itch of need was crawling all over her skin. Instead of complaining, Nikki ran one finger through her folds until she could drive it inside.

"Damn, baby," RJ moaned. He sped up his jacking.

"Don't blow," she said. "I want your cock inside me."

"Yes," he hissed. RJ dropped to his knees next to her.

"You want in me?" she asked, adding a second finger. A quiver shook her body.

"God, yes," he whispered.

Nikki lifted her hips to push in deeper. Damn, the way RJ was watching her work herself just added to the erotic scene. She was powerful and desired.

"Let me," RJ begged, stopping the movement of her hand.

She spread her legs and nodded. "Please."

RJ clasped her hand, lifting it to his mouth and cleaning the juices from her fingers before holding it over her head.

"My turn," he said as he positioned himself between her legs.

"Hurry," she demanded. If he didn't move, Nikki was going to scream.

"I'd planned a romantic evening in front of a fire to show you show much I care about you. But you have me so worked up there's no way I can be gentle."

"I don't want gentle. Not now. You can be romantic later. I promise."

RJ scooted up until the tip of his shaft rested against her folds. He pressed in slowly. Nikki was entranced by the look on his face as he watched his cock pierce her. The feeling of fullness grew until he was buried balls-deep.

"Wrap your legs around my waist," he ordered.

She did so, pushing her shoulders into the ground and making her body bow. "Take me."

RJ withdrew; his grip on her waist almost painful as he filled her.

Perfect, just like the other times they'd been together. He set a brutal pace and she loved it. Yes, it was going to be quick and messy, but she craved what only he could give her. The only person who knew that she wasn't fragile and could handle the roughness.

RJ plunged deep, hard and fast. She was ready, her orgasm hit and she shouted. Even as he continued thrusting, Nikki let her sated body relax. Sweat dripped off RJ's forehead and landed on her cheek. When he came, heat flooded her pussy. She would carry his scent with her for a long while.

Chapter Ten

Doctor Stephanie Adams was not who Nikki had pictured when she'd outlined her series of articles for Dylan to relay to the Council. The beautiful wolf shifter was in her late thirties and already one of the top children's surgeons in the country. Nikki had been thinking of a male shifter in some high-powered profession. That way she could show how much alike they were to the pure humans. Instead, the Council had chosen a specialized doctor who was both known and respected.

This series was going to be even better than Nikki could have dreamed up.

Doctor Adams was going to throw a wrench in all the bigots' hate speech. The five-foot-two, red-haired, green-eyed woman was softly spoken, kind and brilliant. Sitting across the kitchen table from her, Nikki was having trouble not comparing how ordinary she seemed against the doctor. The doctor was classy and beautiful. Nikki was just sort of plain.

She cleared her throat. "I really appreciate you coming here for this," Nikki said. "I would have been more than willing to travel to see you, Doctor Adams."

"Please call me Stephanie, and I wanted to come. It's been a long time since I've been surrounded by so many shifters and, to be honest, it's a nice change. I don't have any family and my Pack was so small that we just sort of all went our separate ways."

"Then I'm happy to be able to offer you a chance to relax and recharge with us." The sadness that came from the doctor was heavy. Something had happened in this woman's life that had her distancing herself from others. The wolf nature inside Nikki couldn't allow a fellow wolf to suffer alone. The Council had told her that Stephanie had volunteered to come and stay for as long as Nikki needed. It was a great opportunity.

"Thank you." Stephanie leaned back in her chair and for the first time looked at ease. She'd arrived the previous night as Nikki and RJ were returning from their camping trip. Brandon had picked her up from the airport and when Nikki had returned home, he hadn't said much about the female shifter other than that she seemed nice.

RJ had tried to help her press Brandon, but her oldest brother had been suspiciously quiet.

"You have a nice home," Stephanie said. "Did you grow up here?"

"Yes, my older brother raised me and my other brother Justin here."

"Oh, the sheriff, right? Brandon."

Is that interest I detect? Which would explain why Brandon wouldn't gossip with her about the doctor. Yep, she'd have to keep an eye on that. Maybe get a little payback on all the teasing she'd gotten when she'd hooked up with RJ. "Yes, he's a good sheriff and even better brother." Nikki had no issues talking Brandon up. Even though she had no interest in his love life, returning home and finding RJ had opened her eyes to what Brandon had sacrificed for her.

"He seemed very kind," Stephanie said with a smile. "Usually people learn about my profession and either try to shmooze me or are too intimated to talk to me. Your brother made me feel like a regular person."

Oh, RJ was going to love hearing this. There was something between the doctor and Brandon. "Brandon has always been down to earth. Coming home always helped me recharge. He just has something about him that allows me to relax."

"Exactly." Stephanie nodded. "But that's not why I was sent here. Can you tell me more about your project? I looked up some of your work before I agreed. Once I saw how talented you were, it helped me feel more comfortable."

"Aren't you afraid this will hurt your career?" She had to ask. As political as she'd seen the medical industry in the past, Nikki couldn't imagine how Stephanie would even think of doing this.

Stephanie laughed. "It crossed my mind. But I decided I needed to pick a side. Since I don't have a Pack, the decision to come out is absolutely mine. I'd considered hiding, but then I'm doing nothing to help those of my kind who've been hurt and killed for what they are."

Nikki leaned forward as she listened. There was something about the way Stephanie spoke that drew Nikki in. "What do you mean, killed?"

"Have you heard of the Clyde Pack of Missouri?" Stephanie asked.

"No."

"I was born there. The Alpha was my uncle. My dad's brother. My father had fourteen siblings. All of my aunts and uncles had at least three children, except for my parents. My dad was the youngest so he'd just started his family. He and my mom had been mated two years before I was born." Stephanie paused to take a drink of her coffee.

"You don't have to talk about this if you don't want to," Nikki assured her. Even though the emotion was the exact one she wanted to capture, it was obvious that Stephanie was hurting just talking about what had happened to her family.

"You need to hear this. If you want to capture the same sentiment in this series as you have in the past, you need to know why I'm doing it."

"Okay," Nikki said. "Go ahead."

"I was three years old the night the hunters came."

"Hunters?" Nikki asked.

Stephanie pressed her lips together. "It seems that one of my cousins met a man who she thought she'd mate with. They'd only been dating about two months, but she told him our secret."

"Werewolf hunters," Nikki stated. The stories of the humans who had once hunted down those of her kind were sparse. From what Nikki could remember, the UK shifters had suffered the most losses. Belief and credence had never really taken off in America.

"Yes," Stephanie said. "The monsters that we thought our parents made up to scare us as children. Except they really existed and they wiped out most of my Pack."

"Your cousin's boyfriend?"

"He told his grandfather, who was a retired hunter. Three days after my cousin spilled the secret, the hunters came. My parents hid me and a few of the Pack who weren't in town. We're the only ones who survived the massacre."

"Why haven't I ever heard about this?" Nikki questioned. "That many people killed?"

"But they weren't people. My family shifted in order to fight the hunters. There was only the corpses of wolves."

"My God!" Nikki exclaimed. "I'm so sorry you went through that."

"As am I."

Both she and Stephanie jumped at Brandon's voice. Nikki looked over to the back door where her brother and RJ had returned from their run.

Stephanie wiped at her tears and Nikki rose.

"You scared the shit out of me," Nikki accused.

"Sorry," Brandon said, brushing past her to kneel close to Stephanie.

"You okay?" RK questioned as he embraced her from behind.

Nikki turned away from where Brandon was comforting to peer up at RJ. "How much did you hear?"

"Enough to know that the doctor has a good reason to want to do this story with you. That was devastating to hear."

"I bet it was worse to go through. She's amazing. After everything that she's been through, she concentrated on her education. She graduated early, fast tracked through medical school and is now one of the most sought-after specialized doctors. I can't imagine how she's managed all of that," Nikki said.

RJ motioned her toward the door. Maybe Stephanie needed a few minutes to collect herself. Nikki sure as hell did. She led the way out, pausing when she reached the steps of the deck. Since most of their serious conversations seemed to take place on a porch, she suspected he wanted to say something he didn't want overheard as well.

"Dylan told me there's more to the reason for why the council suggested the doctor come here instead of you joining her at her apartment on New York," RJ said.

Ah, so I'm right. RJ did know something about why the Council had chosen the doctor. "Why?"

"They're hoping that spending time with this project and around shifters, she'll find the peace of home," RJ said.

"The Council wants her to join our Pack?"

"If she feels comfortable here, yes."

"Why would she want to live in the middle of nowhere when she's a famous surgeon?" Nikki asked.

RJ shrugged. "All I got from Dylan is that after the slaughter of her family, the Council have been watching over her. They raised her in the Council compound until she left for school. They've tried to give her everything she needs, but there's one thing even the Council can't provide for her."

"A family," Nikki guessed.

"Yes. They're hoping we might be the right fit."

Nikki blew out a breath pacing to the body of the steps to sit. RJ pressed against her back, sitting above her.

"Why us?" she asked.

RJ laughed. "That's the same thing I asked. Dylan didn't have an answer for me. He just said the Council believed we could help heal her broken heart."

"It's kind of creepy when they say things like that."

"It is," he agreed. "Does this change anything? Are you

still going to work on the project?"

"Of course I am." Nikki leaned to rest her head on his chest. "I want to do this more now than ever. If we can make sure no one ever has to suffer the way that Stephanie has, then it's our duty to see this through."

He kissed the top of her head. "I think you're pretty amazing as well."

Nikki snorted. "I think you're biased. I've not done anything as remarkable as Stephanie."

"I don't know about that. You've changed my life," RJ said.

She turned to the side so she could see his face. "Are you getting all romantic on me?"

"I've been trying to tell you something for a few days now."

Nikki frowned. "What is it? You can tell me anything."

"Without scaring you away?"

"Of course," Nikki assured him. She might not always say the right thing, but she hoped by now that RJ trusted her.

"Look at me," he demanded.

"I am." Nikki was staring right at him.

"I love you, Nikki."

If she hadn't been watching his lips move, Nikki might have doubted the words he'd spoken. She wanted what RJ had just admitted to be true.

"Say something," he whispered when she'd been silent for too long.

"You love me?" she asked. And wow, that was not what she'd meant to say.

RJ chuckled. "I do."

"Thank God!" Nikki pushed up until she was straddling RJ. "I love you, too."

"I'm really glad you said that. You had me worried."

"Sorry. I just wanted to savor the first time you told me. Make sure I really heard you right."

"You heard me," RJ said. "I'm ready to start my future with you."

"Yes," Nikki agreed. "Our future."

* * * *

Nikki raised the camera and took several shots in quick succession. Stephanie appeared almost angelic, standing over the small girl she was examining. It wasn't what she specialized in, but she was still a medical doctor and had begun to volunteer at the local medical center. Which was great for Nikki since this gave her an opportunity to see Stephanie at work. And capture the scene, just as she was currently doing.

It'd been two days and she had hundreds of pictures for this second piece of her series, but she hadn't captured the right moment yet.

The little patient giggled as Stephanie ticked her tummy while checking for tenderness.

There it was. The girl reaching up to embrace her doctor as Stephanie whispered words of reassurance to her.

"Perfect," Nikki murmured.

* * * *

RJ tossed the newspaper containing Nikki's second article onto the counter of his shop before strolling over to the mini fridge. He couldn't believe the amount of attention that her series was generating. He'd suspected her work would help their cause, but they'd seen both an outpouring of support and almost the same amount of threats.

Their town was never going to be the same again.

Not that the changes were all bad. They'd accepted several new members of the Pack as well as providing a safe place for others until they moved on. So much had changed in the three months since the announcement and RJ was thrilled.

The bell on the front door sounded, drawing his attention. Nikki strolled in with her hands full. RJ rushed over to grab the bags from her. The scent of spicy orange chicken wafted up.

"Chinese food?"

"And beer," she said, holding up a six pack.

"Fancy, what's the occasion?"

Nikki laughed, the sound light and flowing. "I have a favor to ask."

RJ moaned. In the month since they'd moved into the apartment above his shop, a favor ranged from replacing a light bulb to stripping and restaining the floors. He never knew what was going on in that brilliant head of hers.

"Oh, don't be that way," she said. "You didn't mind last night when I wanted to break in the new chair."

"And while I enjoyed that, I have a feeling this isn't going to consist of you and me naked on brown suede."

She shook her head while reaching to the counter to set down the drinks. Nikki picked up the newspaper. "Did you read it?"

"Of course, and it was even better than the first one."

"I had to turn my cell off. It wouldn't stop ringing. Brandon said that the house phone hasn't stopped either with people wanting to talk to Stephanie."

RJ smiled. Nikki's brother had fallen hard and fast for the doctor. After only two weeks at the hotel in town, Stephanie had started staying with Brandon and hadn't left yet. Brandon had moved his over-protectiveness from Nikki to the doctor, which made Nikki happy. RJ, on the other hand, had to be on constant watch in case any of Nikki's articles resulted in someone coming after her. "I bet Brandon's about ready to strangle someone."

"Yeah, I had to get out of the house. I've almost finished packing up my old room. Probably just a couple of hours more."

"You know you can keep some stuff there," RJ told her. "You don't have to move everything into storage."

"It's time. Brandon hasn't ever gotten rid of anything of mine and Justin's. I don't want to throw it away, so storage for now. We'll decide what to do with it later."

"And the stuff from your apartment in Houston?"

"Be here at the end of the week," she responded.

That was the last of what they needed to be officially living together, even though they never spent one night apart. RJ was certain he'd feel even better once her things were mixed in with his. There were times when RJ still wondered if he would be enough.

Nikki shrugged out of her jacket and dropped it onto a chair then opened the plastic bag holding their dinner containers. "Sit."

RJ plopped down into the other chair as she pulled out the food boxes and beer bottles. He waited until she was sitting next to him. "The favor?"

"I want a tattoo." She didn't even glance at him when she made the request, just dug her fork into the fried rice.

"I'm sorry?"

"I saw your sketch book," she said. "You left it open on the kitchen table last night."

RJ knew exactly what she was talking about. It was something he'd been working on for over a month. "How do you know that's for you?"

She snorted. "The pen is mightier than the sword? Really?"

"You don't know all my clients," he pointed out.

"Fine. Be that way."

He let her sit and eat, knowing that she wasn't finished.

By the time she'd started her second beer, she was shaking her leg, unable to sit still. She was ready to burst.

"So who's the tattoo for?" she finally asked.

"When it's finished, it'll be for you," he admitted.

She beamed. "I knew it! But why do I have to wait? It looks great."

"It's not finished. And I won't rush it. It has to be perfect if it's going to be on your body."

Nikki nodded. "But who will I ever get to ink me?"

RJ gripped her shoulder and tugged her closer. "Like I would let anyone else put their hands on you. I see many more tattoos in your future and every one of them will be done by my hand."

"But who'll do yours?" she asked. The way she angled herself to look at him, he didn't think this subject was something she'd just thought of.

"I normally draw my own and have one of the guys ink it."

"So it's something that can be taught?" she asked.

"Of course," he replied. "Do you want to learn?"

The way her face lit up surprised him. He hadn't known that she'd had any interest in his art form. It would be great to share this with her.

"So if you started working on our matching tattoos, I could do yours?" she whispered.

"Matching?" RJ sucked in his breath. "Are you saying what I think you are?"

"You specialize in mating tattoos, right?"

His heart was pounding and his palms were damp. "Yes."

"And if I wanted to wait and have that be my first?"

"They'd have to be perfect," he told her. RJ meant what he said about not allowing anything less than perfect on her body.

"It's a good thing that you've already started, then, right?"

RJ thought about the sketch pad that he kept under the counter. There was no way Nikki would have seen that unless she'd been snooping. He made sure never to work on that when she was around. RJ didn't want to put any pressure on her, even though all he wanted with every fiber of his being was to mate with her. "What makes you think that I've already started?"

She rose and sauntered over to the counter. When she reached down and picked up the right book, he simply raised his brow.

"Oh, like you're surprised. I've been through every inch of this place."

"Well, it is your home now," he stated.

"Yes, it is." She set his pad down before wrapping her arm around his neck. "And this is where we'll start out mated life together."

RJ wasn't prepared for this conversation. He downed the rest of his beer and eyed hers close by.

"Hey." She cupped his face. "What is it?"

Fuck it. He grabbed Nikki's beer and finished it off.

"RJ?" Nikki backed off. "I thought you wanted to mate. I didn't mean to assume."

"You didn't," he said. "I want that more than anything."

"Then what's wrong?"

It was hard to say, but he had to be fair to both of them. "Mating is forever. If we commit ourselves that way, there's no turning back."

"I'm aware of that," she said. "Do you really think I'd go into this if I had any doubts?"

"You might not have doubts now, but what about in five years? Or ten? How long do you think you'll be happy here until you want to move on?" RJ questioned. A tightness in his chest started and he rubbed at the pain.

Nikki shook her head. "I'm pretty sure I should be insulted, but I understand your concern. This doesn't change who I am. Just where I call home."

"I can't leave my brother's side," RJ told her. "Not now and probably not even when things settle down. As an Alpha, he'll always need someone to watch his back. I don't trust anyone else to do it."

"And my family is here as well," she said. "I understand your concern, but I've worked this out. Yes, there will be times that I have to travel, but I'll always come home and to you."

"You promise?"

"What's more, I plan to change how I accept assignments and projects," she stated.

"How?"

"The Council is very pleased with how this series is going." She tapped her nails against the newspaper.

"Because it's brilliant."

"Thank you." She kissed his cheek. "But now that the

shifters have become public, they've asked me to work for them. To showcase the lives, struggles, triumphs and more of the shifter kind."

"Is that something you want to do?" RJ hoped he didn't sound as excited as he felt. He didn't want her to take this on just for him.

"I think so," she told him. "There are still some details to work out, but I'd be able to do more for our people. I've spent my entire career trying to help bring to light the problems of the world. Now it's time I took care of the ones I love the most."

"I'm proud of you," RJ praised.

"So you'll consider mating with me?"

"Oh, baby." RJ tugged her into his lap. "There is nothing to consider. You're mine and of course I'll mate with you."

She peppered his face with kisses as tears filled her eyes.

RJ caught her chin, brought her mouth to his and put into the press of his lips all the words that he couldn't get out. Nikki Stratton, the woman who'd stormed into his life and turned everything upside down was now his.

Nikki was shaking by the time they separated. "I guess, as you're the brother of the Alpha, we'll have to have an official ceremony."

"Oh, I'm sure that Dylan will insist on it." RJ rose with her still in his arms. "That doesn't mean we can't start practicing."

She giggled and clutched at him. "After we practice, maybe we can talk about those tattoos."

"You got it," RJ said. "Maybe I'll even show you the updated sketch you didn't find."

"Wait! What?"

RJ smacked her ass, causing her to squeal and jump. "You haven't seen my latest that I keep in my backpack."

"You've been holding out on me," she accused.

"No," he corrected. "You just shouldn't have been snooping."

Still carrying her, he locked the front door to the shop

before striding across to the stairs that led to their living quarters. Prior to Mike leaving, he'd helped RJ repaint the area and, with the assistance of Ben, they'd managed to secure the perfect furniture to make the small but tidy space special.

The look on Nikki's face when he'd presented their work to her had been magical. He hoped that one day they'd have a house with enough room for a family, but for the time being he liked living in the middle of town above his shop.

RJ could still keep an ear out for any trouble as well as keep Nikki close.

Half the apartment had been dedicated to a workspace in order for Nikki to be able to do her work.

As RJ carried Nikki to the bedroom, his mind raced through all the possibilities for him and Nikki. Being Pack mates was only the beginning of their connection. Mating would seal the bond. But it was love that would keep them together.

Pack Community

Excerpt

Chapter One

Early evening heat surrounded Gray Mason as he stepped out of his Ford truck after pulling over to the side of the road. The sign in front of him welcomed him to Coyote Bluff, Texas, located in the panhandle of the large state, a place he had never visited before. But recent signs had narrowed down the location of Prince of felines to a couple of possibilities — one of them being the canyons surrounding the town.

After he'd spoken to the Alpha Council and the Pack Alpha for the west Texas area, arrangements had been made for Gray to investigate in Coyote Bluff. He'd been hearing rumors about the town that accepted any and all shifters since he'd begun to investigate the kidnapping. It would make since for whoever had taken the Prince to hide out in an area that was so remote.

Excitement rippled through his body at the thought of the search finally going somewhere after three very long months. While the idea of an entire town full of shifters unsettled him a bit, he would do everything in his power to finally end his journey and make his way home.

He surveyed the area directly around him, seeking anyone who might be a threat. Sensing no one near, he took out his cell phone and called his Alpha.

"Hey, Gray, I was starting to wonder if I'd hear from you today," Tyler greeted him.

Gray had to smile. Tyler would worry whether Gray called in or not, but Gray liked knowing that someone would at least notice if he went missing.

"Yeah, sorry about that, boss," Gray answered and leaned against his tailgate. "Crappy reception down here."

"Just be careful. I contacted the sheriff there to let him know you would be stopping by in a day or so. He seems like an okay guy, but remember we don't have any ties there," Tyler warned.

"So he's not family?" Gray enquired, asking his Alpha in this way if the man was a wolf shifter.

"I don't think so. The town is supposed to be full of other shifters, but I just can't tell over the phone."

Gray grunted. It wasn't that he didn't like the others — he just hadn't met many. Most of his dealings were with the felines and those experiences had not been good.

"I'll check into the hotel tonight, get a run in and see what I can nose out before I meet with him tomorrow," Gray informed the other man.

"Just be careful. There is no wolf Pack there, but that doesn't mean that there are no wolves. You don't want to trespass against them before you know who you are dealing with. Especially without back-up."

"No problem. I'll stay away from any marked spots."

"Then call me tomorrow and get some rest," Tyler ordered.

"Will do." Gray hung up, still grinning. He had been away

from his Pack for so long he was started to feel the loneliness more and more each day. While some wolf shifters had no problem going rogue, the true, deep comfort he found with his Pack mates had started to fade and it made him edgy. And an agitated wolf was never a good thing. He needed his family. He needed to get home soon.

Normally, he only shifted a few nights a month to let his animal out. The longer he was away from family, the more agitated both he and the wolf became. Running late at night seemed to be the only way he could calm himself, and even that didn't work like it had.

"Coyote Bluff," he mumbled under his breath as he climbed back into his truck. "Out of all the animals who in the world would pick a coyote to name a town after?" Gray didn't know any coyote shifters, although he was aware they existed. Rumor had it that coyote shifters were more than a little crazy. If he had time maybe he'd be able to dig into the history of the place. Gray loved learning about different communities and their unique quirks.

He pulled back onto the main road and followed directions on signs until he found what he'd been looking for. The hotel had the appearance of an old cabin from the pioneer days. He parked in front of the door and got out, pleasantly surprised to see that while it might seem old, it was a sturdy building. The railings spreading from the entrance to both sides were composed of thick pieces of wood with delicate carvings.

A closer look revealed that the carvings were of several different animals. The detail—each species practically came to life—was simply amazing. There seemed to be more to this town than he'd first thought. That boded well for his purpose here.

He hefted his bag over his shoulder and pushed open the large oak door. The spacious entrance seemed to invite him in and Gray found himself smiling.

What greeted him first was the scent of fresh cooking. He'd been living out of convenience stores and on fast food for so long that his mouth watered as he thought about a hot, home-cooked meal. His stomach rumbled in agreement.

"I guess that means the first order of business will be getting you something to eat," a tall, slender woman said, coming to his side, laughing.

Gray grinned at the pretty middle-aged woman. "Didn't realize I was so hungry until I smelt whatever that delicious food is."

The woman laughed again, throwing her head back. "Oh no, Claude does all the cooking around here. But I will tell him you said that. I'm guessing you're Mr. Mason?" she asked and guided him to the small, neat reception desk he hadn't noticed. "I'm Dorothy. Claude and I own this place, so if you need anything, you just give me a holler."

"Yes, ma'am. Gray Mason here to check in and hopefully check out dinner."

"Oh, I am going to like you, Mr. Gray Mason," she told him, patting his hand. "Just sign this registration form. We will charge your credit card when you check out. The dining room is open from five in the morning to eight at night. But if you want anything when it's not open, you just let me know and I'll show you around the kitchen. It's open to all our guests. We get a lot of business in the dining room from the town folk, so don't you worry about what time you eat. We've got plenty to feed everyone."

Gray nodded and signed the paper she'd given him. The heavy welcome card he slid back across the counter to Dorothy reminded him of the old paper his grandparents had enjoyed. The pleasant memory brought him a touch of his past. What an unexpected gem he'd found in this odd town. "If all your food smells like this, I don't see myself eating anywhere else," he said. He had a feeling the meals there would also remind him of a time he'd never get back.

"There are places to grab food in town, also. We have a café, a coffee shop, a bakery, the pizza joint and even a steak house on the other side of town heading out. All good food, although no one cooks like my Claude."

"Now, Dorothy, I think you may be a little biased." Gray turned as a heavyset man joined them. He smiled and seemed friendly, but it was the power behind his eyes that told Gray much about him.

This was a shifter. Not wolf or feline, but something just as powerful. Gray stiffened and faced the man directly. He had hoped to avoid any display of dominance.

The smile fell from the other man's lips as he held out his hand. "Claude Gentry."

"Gray Mason, and Dorothy is correct. It smells amazing," Gray told Claude as they shook. While his wolf might have been straining to get out, Gray was professional enough to control his instincts. Being a detective in a very human world had tested him enough.

As soon as the words left his lips, he felt the change in the other man. Instead of a mood to match the cautious handshake, the man returned to his joyful self. "Well, thank you, son. Let Dorothy get you checked in so we can feed you," he told Gray with a friendly slap on his back.

Gray looked back to the woman in time to see her send Claude a worried glance before smiling at him once more. Gray breathed in deeply, trying to place any familiar scents. The woman was human, although she smelled like Claude. But he just couldn't place the other man. The scent was more fresh air and fields than the wild and woodsy scent of wolves.

He couldn't come right out and ask without sounding rude, so he just pushed it to the back of his mind as he accepted his room key and listened to the directions to his room.

Passing through the cabin — he no longer thought of it as a hotel — he appreciated the beauty and comfort of the décor and feel. He liked the little place already.

His room was located on the second floor, which suited him fine. He wasn't usually picky but being in a strange place surrounded by so many different scents had him on edge. Being on the third or fourth floor would have put him farther away from escape.

Later, maybe after my run, I'll calculate how many exits will get me to safety if need be.

When he reached his room, Gray took a minute to breath in the scents around his door. He didn't catch that any other shifters had passed by recently. Dorothy's pleasant aroma was all he found. Relaxing a little more, Gray put the key in the lock before pushing open his door. It amused him that the cabin didn't use the key cards most hotels had switched over to.

Stepping inside the space that would be his home for the near future, he nodded in approval. Clean and comfortable. There might not have been a lot of furniture—just a large bed, a couple of night stands, desk with chair and a long dresser—but it would suit his needs.

Instead of unpacking, Gray wanted to get back down to the dining room. He'd really grown hungry and it had been a long drive.

He dropped his bag onto the bottom of the bed then spun around to stroll right back out of the door.

Gray reached the bottom of the stairs and found Dorothy standing there, apparently waiting for him.

"I didn't think it would take you long to head back down here, so I had Claude start making you a plate," she said.

"I appreciate it, ma'am."

"Now." She waved her hand. "None of that. We're family here. You just call me Dorothy."

"Only if you call me Gray."

"It will be my pleasure," she said. Dorothy threaded her arm through his, urging him to the entrance of the dining hall.

There were already several couples eating who checked him out when Dorothy escorted him in. A few glanced up but only smiled before returning to their meals. Gray was taken back by the easy acceptance from other shifters.

He'd really underestimated Coyote Bluff.

"Now, you sit here by the window. As the sun sets, you'll

have a great view of our wonderful town," Dorothy told him when they'd reached the spot she wanted him to take.

"Sounds perfect." Gray pulled out the chair and sat before Dorothy could do it for him.

"Now what do you prefer to drink?"

"An ice tea would be perfect."

"Sweet or unsweet?"

Gray laughed. "In Texas? I'm going to go with the sweet tea."

Beaming, she patted his shoulder. "Good man."

She was off in a flash, surprising him. Dorothy moved quickly, almost as if she floated.

Movement in the corner of his eye caught his attention and he leaned forward, trying to see what it was. A small animal darted between two cars, but he couldn't tell what it had been.

"Here you go, Gray." Dorothy set down his glass then a plate full of barbecue ribs, potato salad, green beans with bacon and cornbread.

"Oh, my God!" He bent forward, breathing deeply. He hadn't even ordered, but Dorothy had brought him exactly what he'd been craving.

"Enjoy!" Dorothy told him before leaving him to his overflowing plate.

Gray dug in, concentrating on filling his stomach with the best food he'd ever tasted. If anyone was watching, they'd probably think he hadn't eaten in months and Gray wouldn't have blamed them. He barely took the time to swallow. It was so fucking good.

Dorothy stopped by once to refill his tea while looking pleased with his progress.

It wasn't until he lifted his head that he noticed most of the other patrons had finished and left. The sun wasn't completely down, but it was most definitely dusk.

"You ate every bit," Dorothy commented with pride. "That will make Claude very happy."

"You must tell him that I enjoyed every bite. Best food

I've eaten in years."

"I'll do that." She set down a bottle of domestic beer. "Now why don't you take this and sit out on the porch. Take in the sights and relax."

Gray stood and kissed her cheek, letting impulse take him over. He wasn't naturally a touchy-feely kind of guy, but the moment seemed to call for it.

"You'll fit in her perfectly." She patted his face and, if he wasn't mistaken, her eyes were damp. "Just perfectly."

Gray nodded, feeling embarrassed by his actions, before picking up his beer. He high-tailed it out of the dining room toward the side entrance where he'd spotted some nice-looking wooden seating.

Despite the name, Coyote Bluff was a gorgeous town. He always felt better being surrounded by the woods and forests of home, but the canyons that surrounded him now had their own charm. He couldn't wait until later when he would be able to change forms and run.

But for now, as he waited for the evening to pass, he dropped down into one of the many chairs on the porch and kicked back. The restlessness that he had felt since before he'd arrived calmed and peace settled deep inside him until his eyes started to droop and he let himself drift.

It was the light sound of footsteps that kicked his instincts into gear and had him popping his lids back open. Just off to the side at the porch steps stood a little boy, about five or six, staring at him.

Gray dropped his feet onto the deck and nodded in the kid's direction.

Taking that as an invitation, the little boy scrambled up the steps to hover over him. "I'm Julian, I live next door, my aunt said I could come over and get some cookies from Claude, he makes really good cookies and he always saves me some."

The words flew so fast and with such a heavy southern accent that Gray actually had to think about what had been said. Once he put it all together, he grinned. His Alpha had a young daughter, so he'd had some dealings with small children. "I haven't had the cookies yet, but I hope you'll save me one."

The boy started to nod immediately. "I will. I promise."

Before Gray could respond, the boy scrunched up his face and sniffed. He knew the child was scenting him and, while it would have been rude from an adult, he had a feeling the young boy he had just met didn't worry about things like that. Discreetly, he breathed in the boy's scent as well.

He was shocked to smell cat.

"You smell funny!" Julian told him, leaning closer.

Gray couldn't hold in a laugh at the boy's exclamation and puzzled face. Once he quieted down, he knew that no matter what species Julian was, the kid was all right. "I don't think I smell that bad. I took a shower earlier," he teased.

This caused Julian to shake his head so quickly he almost fell over. "No, you don't smell bad—just funny."

So he hadn't smelled another wolf before. That was interesting.

"Well, I'm a wolf, so maybe that's it," Gray offered.

And found himself with a lap full of kid.

"You're a wolf!" Julian squealed. "A wolf! That is so cool! I always wanted to meet a wolf. Daddy says that when I'm bigger I'll be able to meet everyone, but right now it's not safe."

Gray took in the boy's pout and pleading eyes and patted his back reassuringly. "You should listen to your dad—he seems like a smart guy. And right now it may not be safe, but hopefully when you're bigger it will be."

"But you're a good wolf, right? You won't eat me or anything?"

Gray forced back another chuckle. "No, I promise I won't eat you."

The child relaxed in his lap. "That's cool then. What's your name? Did you tell me already? I don't remember you telling me, but sometimes I don't listen too well."

"I think I might have forgotten to tell you. My name is Gray."

"Gray?" Julian chewed on his lip. "I like that. Is it because in your other form you're gray?"

It was a good question and kind of made Gray proud of the boy, which surprised him because the child was still a complete stranger. A feline. Oh well, he could puzzle over that later. Right now he was enjoying his new friend.

"Actually, I'm not gray at all as a wolf."

"Huh?" Julian thought about that.

"Well, little man? What are you?" Gray finally asked.

"Oh!" Julian jumped down so fast he almost toppled them both. But then he balled his hands on his hips and stuck his chest out. "I'm a bobcat!"

"Really?" Gray wouldn't have guessed that. Maybe that was why Julian's scent was a little different from the other felines he'd encountered. He had never met a bobcat before. Lions and one tiger, but Julian was his first bobcat, so Gray told him that.

"Really!" The kid squealed again. "That's so totally awesome!"

"Julian Jameson Williams!"

The boy and Gray both started as a woman rushed up the steps.

"I am so sorry, mister. I didn't know he was out here pestering you. He was supposed to run into the kitchen and be right back," she hurriedly told him, pulling Julian to her side.

Gray stood almost knocked back by the woman's beauty. She was probably in her early thirties, with bright green eyes and reddish blonde hair. She was quite a bit shorter than him and with her curvy body and ample breasts, he was embarrassed to find himself getting hard.

She stood in front of him in nothing fancier than old jeans and a tank top and he wanted to pounce on her. He took a step back just to be safe. It had been so long since he'd been that attracted to anyone.

"It's fine, really. I enjoyed visiting with Julian," he told her.

She smiled then, relaxing just a touch, and it took his breath away. The fact that the female had the scent of a cat didn't seem to bother his body or his wolf, who scratched to get out and play.

"Aunt Beth! Gray is a good wolf! He promised not to eat me," Julian told his aunt with all the innocence that could only come from one so small.

"Oh my! He didn't!" she exclaimed, hand going to her mouth.

Gray chuckled to show her he wasn't offended. "Yes, I did promise that and I always keep my promises, buddy."

Julian grinned back and finally the woman laughed.

"You'll have to excuse us. We haven't dealt with…with your…kind much," she stumbled, trying to explain.

Gray waved her off. "I understand. This is new for me, too. Julian is my first bobcat."

"Aunt Beth is a bobcat, too!" Julian added helpfully.

Gray had figured that but was glad to have it confirmed to him. That way he could get his head around the fact that, while she might be the sweetest-looking thing, she was still a cat and therefore still suspect.

"I thought I heard voices out here," Claude said, joining them on the porch. He carried a small plastic bag with him. "Beth called over to send Julian back, but I hadn't seen him. I take it you both have met our new guest?"

"Yes, Claude! And he's a wolf. But a nice wolf. He won't eat me."

Claude glanced over at Gray, who just nodded. Okay, it had been funny at first, but now he was starting to worry about all the wolf talk. He hoped it wasn't the same around town or he would never be able to get anything useful from the residents.

And he needed to find something there. They needed a lead.

Claude handed over the bag and Julian immediately dug

in.

"Just one for now," Beth admonished.

Julian took one out then peered up at his aunt. "One for each hand?"

Beth shook her head before laughing. "No."

"Okay." Julian turned to him and held out the plastic sack. "One for me and one for my new friend."

Gray was touched. "That's very kind of you. Thank you, Julian." He selected the smallest treat so that Julian would get his fill later.

"You're welcome!" Julian exclaimed.

"We'd better get going." Beth tugged on Julian's arm.

"Bye, Mr. Wolf!"

"Good night, Julian." He dipped his head. "Ma'am."

"Night," Beth said quietly before her and Julian walked back down the stairs.

Gray watched for only a few seconds, aware that Claude was still by his side.

"He's a cute kid," Gray said.

Claude chuckled. "Julian's a handful and it takes all of us to keep that boy out of trouble, but he is also a gentle soul. I'm sorry if he disturbed you."

"He didn't," Gray assured the older man. "I enjoyed our visit."

"Good." Claude straightened his shoulders. "You were also very kind to Dorothy. I appreciate it."

Why do these people keep thanking me for being a decent person? What kind of wolf shifter have they met before? "Dorothy made me feel welcome and the meal was fantastic. I've been away from home a long time and this is the first time I've smiled and laughed in months. Everyone has been welcoming. I'm the appreciative one."

Claude gave him a firm nod before he slipped back inside.

Okay, things might not be as perfect in Coyote Bluff as he'd started to think. Which was a bit of a comfort since he was almost ready to claim them all to be some sort of pod people.

Gray retook his seat and kicked his feet back up onto the rail. He could barely see the porch of the house next door. Somewhere inside, Julian was probably eating his cookies with Beth. Gray wished he could've joined him. And didn't that bear some serious thinking?

Beth led Julian up the stairs to the second floor and his room, still thinking about the wolf shifter. It'd scared her to death when she had spotted her nephew right in front of the man. Every protective instinct she had in her had wanted to jump in front of the boy until the threat was gone.

Instead, she had been stunned at how open and friendly he had been. Not to mention handsome. Even as she'd crossed the yard, desire had battled her fear. But she couldn't afford to think like that. While her community might be built on tolerance of human and inter-species relationships, she was still a cat and he a wolf. Sometimes it wasn't meant to be, and, attracted or not, this was one of those times.

Well, maybe she could still think about those gorgeous eyes that had practically set her on fire. His built body and height hadn't hurt, either. *No one has to know, do they?* If he had been a cat, or any other species, she would have thought he'd make the perfect mate.

She sighed inwardly as Julian went on and on about the wolf next door. She would have to warn her brother that Julian was completely taken with the stranger. When Julian's naturally curious nature came out and he got this way, only time would divert his attention.

Together, the two of them followed Julian's nightly ritual of brushing teeth and getting ready for bed. Once her nephew was tucked in, she kissed his forehead. "Daddy will be home soon and in to check on you," she told him.

"Cool! I'll tell him all about my new friend!"

She smiled down at him, although she had every intention of beating him to it. That way, at least her brother would be a little more prepared than she had been.

Back downstairs, she made herself a glass of iced sweet

tea and went to sit on the front porch swing. Her body still hummed happily after the encounter with the wolf shifter and, although she couldn't act on it, she thought she might as well enjoy it while she could.

Few wolves ever ventured into Coyote Bluff. Wolves tended to keep with their Packs and in their territory. The ones that had come by usually didn't last long. They were too dominating to leave things alone around the place, and while the people might be tolerant of one another, they were also protective. Their ways worked for them. And no one was going to let a rogue wolf come in and take over. A few had tried, but they were almost always quickly run out of town.

With the exception of one wolf, none had ever stayed. Mark was a special case, though. The wolf was so tormented and afraid that he jumped at his own shadow. Even after a year of living in town, the wolf had hardly ever left his house and, as far as she knew, had never shifted. She wasn't completely sure what had happened to him and she never pressed. They had become friends, but she knew she was one of only a few. Julian had never met Mark.

The story about the feline Prince being taken had reached them when it happened. The town wasn't into the politics of the felines and others, but given the number of felines in town, they'd been asked to keep an eye out for anything suspicious. The rumor of the wolves helping search for him seemed to be true, if the reason for Gray's visit was really an attempt to assist with the rescue.

The sheriff, Joe, had told them that some of the searchers might be coming down, but Beth hadn't really thought any other shifter species would care about the Prince. Half of her own species didn't care. Cats were solitary creatures and while they did have a royal line that governed the big laws, most felines lived their own lives and didn't get involved in one another's business. It wasn't that way here in Coyote Bluff, though. The closeness of the community was what she appreciated about her home. She could live close to her family and wasn't expected to fend for herself. Very un-cat-like.

Her brother, Dawson, and Julian were the only close family members she had. Their parents had left them right after they had become adults. The oldest sibling—her and Dawson's brother, Casey—had joined the military and they hadn't seen him since. That had been twenty years ago. Luckily Dawson also felt the same way about having family close by, or she would be alone.

The headlights from her brother's patrol car bathed her in a spotlight as he parked. She scooted over on the swing as he stomped the dust off his boots then took a seat next to her.

"It's a nice night. I thought the heat would never break," he greeted.

It had been unusually hot for May. Already hitting the hundreds and summer wasn't even upon them yet.

She handed over her tea to share and nudged his shoulder. "Julian made a new friend."

Relaxing back into the wood swing, Dawson chuckled. "What is it this time? A fish in the pond or maybe a rat from the barn?"

Julian forever made friends with anything that moved. Shifter or regular animal, it didn't matter.

"Wolf shifter," she said quietly.

Dawson stiffened and paused, seeming to think about his words before he spoke.

"So he made it to town? Joe wasn't sure what day, but had thought within three."

She nodded. "Came in tonight. I didn't know he had arrived yet and Julian wanted some of Claude's cookies."

"And instead found a wolf?" Dawson guessed.

"Yep. When he didn't come right back, I went looking for him and found him on the porch of the inn."

Dawson inhaled—his way of getting himself to keep calm. She should probably stop teasing him, but what were sisters for?

"Damn it, Beth." His patience was finally up. "Do I need to kick a wolf's ass or not?"

Giggling, she slapped her brother's leg. "Nah, he promised not to eat Julian."

Dawson groaned. "Please tell me he didn't use those exact words."

"Oh, he sure did."

"Damn it," he groused. "I never would have said that if I'd known Julian would take it so literally."

She snorted, unable to hold back her amusement. "Well, Gray seemed pretty cool about it, if that helps."

Shaking his head, he stood. "If he's here for more than a few days, I can only imagine what else will be said. But I guess I'll find out tomorrow. Joe wants me to show Gray some of the trails. We don't think anyone has been past the barriers into the unused parts of the canyon, but really it's too big to know for sure. The park rangers are covering the public entrances."

"Is that why he's here? He thinks someone might be hiding in the canyon?" Usually her brother kept work to himself, but if he was willing to talk, she wanted to know. She had the same curious nature as her nephew.

"It's nothing to worry about," Dawson told her, switching back to 'big brother'. "If anyone is here, we'll find them for sure. It's been a long hot day. I'm going to work out before I shower."

"Okay. Now that it's cooled down, I might go for a run."

"Just be careful. Especially with a strange wolf in town."

"I promise not to be eaten by the big bad wolf, either," she teased.

Dawson rolled his eyes but went into the house without saying anything further. It was a good thing, because once she caught her own words, she blushed, thinking about one way she wouldn't mind being eaten by the wolf.

She sighed and set her tea down on the table. A run was a good idea. She could burn off some energy and hopefully not be up all night thinking about the sexy man next door.

Trails to the canyon area were all over town. It gave the residents easy access to let their animal sides loose. The public access to the canyon was on the other side of the area, with hundreds of acres in between. Even if they were spotted as animals, no one would be the wiser. And she could smell the humans before they would ever see her. Plus, the park rangers kept all bridges and roads to their area closed off. It helped that most of the rangers were shifters or related to one somehow.

That was how the community worked. They watched out for one another. Humans had the police. The shifters only had each other.

It was a short ten-minute walk to the clearing where she could shift. She climbed up and into the cave she and Dawson used, quickly shedding her clothes before becoming a bobcat.

She stretched, enjoying the pull on her muscles. Even though it had been less than a week since she'd shifted, it felt as though it had been much longer. She rubbed against the walls of the cave, giving in to the instinct to mark her territory. There were no other bobcats in the community other than her brother – and when he finally shifted, her nephew – but it still felt good to her cat to follow tradition.

Since she didn't actually like to run, but was more of a climber, she decided to head up to the top of the canyon so she could lie around under the moon. There was a small creek close by, too.

She started up, leaping and jumping as much as she could. Her curious nephew always asked how she felt when she got to shift, and as hard as she tried, she could never find the right words. It felt freeing, as if she was finally completely herself.

The thick foliage covered her as she stalked around, wishing for a playmate to pounce on. Sometimes her brother would come with her, but most of the time she was alone. Even other cats in town preferred to be by themselves. Her cat seemed to be missing that part of its personality.

A low tree branch offered her more fun as she climbed and chewed on it. As she started to scratch, she heard the yowl of a lone wolf not too far from where she was playing.

Planning on just getting a look at the wolf, she leaped from the branch and prowled toward the sound. It was less than five minutes before she caught a woodsy scent ahead of her. Crouching, she started crawling forward.

There, at the creek she had planned on visiting, stood a fully grown wolf. Her senses told her it was also a shifter, but she would have guessed that even without them since she knew how rare that type of wolf was. The red wolves were an endangered species, reported to total less than one hundred in America.

Looking at the animal, she was awed.

She squatted low to the ground to keep her hiding place as he dipped his head to drink from the clear water. *What a beautiful creature*, she mused as he stretched his neck back and howled again. Even though she was a cat, she still felt the loneliness that call conveyed. An answering rumble gathered in her throat and she had to hold herself back.

In the wild they were natural enemies. Even while human, she had never met a wolf who hadn't thought he was better than her.

With a heavy sigh, she laid her head down on the ground. She must have been louder than she'd thought, because his head snapped in her direction. She remained downwind so she knew he hadn't picked up her scent.

She tried to make herself as small as possible, belatedly realizing that spying on a wolf she didn't know wasn't the brightest idea she'd ever had.

To his credit, he didn't charge her. Instead, he tilted his head to the side and lowered himself much the same way she had.

She watched as he slowly crawled closer to her. When their gazes met, he stopped.

The same pull she had felt earlier returned and her muscles bunched as she waited.

He started toward her again, just as slowly and carefully, and she also scooted closer. They had started several yards away, but all too soon—and yet not soon enough—they were in the open with just a few feet separating them.

The wolf rolled to his side and pawed the ground. If she could have, she would have laughed. Instead the sound that came out of her was more of a small purr.

The wolf's ears perked up before he did it again.

So, as he'd asked, she moved to rest next to him. They didn't touch—just breathed in each other and shared the night. Side by side they stayed as the stars over them twinkled and the canyon sounds sang for them.

It was nice—peaceful, even—and she relaxed enough to close her eyes.

A whisper of a hot breath passed over her as the wolf bumped her chin with his head. She nuzzled into him without thinking.

The zing of awareness that shot through her body shocked her. He must have felt something too, because he jerked before nudging her again.

If they were in human form, she had no doubt they would be kissing. But as animals...

She jerked away. Damn it, she was a bobcat. There was no way she could have these feelings for a wolf. As carefully as she could, she inched away from him. He flopped back onto his stomach, watching her.

As he moved toward her, she swiped at him with her claws still sheathed. She didn't want to hurt him, but she had to get away.

What in the world had she been thinking? They hadn't just been playing—they were flirting, practically making out.

Once she had enough room to flee, she turned and took off. She didn't even glance behind her. Didn't dare. She just ran.

She scrambled down the canyon cliffs, not slowing until she got to her cave. Just as she reached her spot, she heard the heart-breaking sound of that howl.

Doesn't matter, she told herself. *We're from two different worlds.*

More books from Crissy Smith

Book one in the Were Chronicles series

Marissa Boyd finds herself drawn into a world she can never be a part of, complete with an Alpha wolf who takes whatever he wants. And he wants her.

Book four in the Were Chronicles series

The Rogue meets the Alpha…and their worlds explode.

Book one in the Bloodlines series

If trouble doesn't come to him, he'll find it on his own.

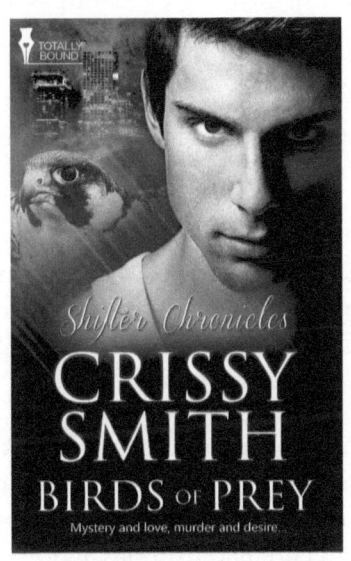

Book one in the Shifter Chronicles series

Mystery and love, murder and desire… It's going to be a rough week for the agents of the Birds of Prey shifter division.

About the Author

Crissy Smith

Crissy Smith lives in Texas with her husband, daughter, and three Labrador retrievers. The three dogs love to curl up under her computer desk and nap while she writes. It doesn't leave a lot of room for her but what's a woman to do?

When not writing or reading, she enjoys hunting, camping and shooting. But she has a girly side too and is addicted to pedicures and coffee.

She has been writing since she was a teenager and still loves everything to do with the paranormal. Her stories and characters all have a place in her heart. She loves the alpha male, the dominant werewolf, or the Master vampire which find their way in most of her books.

Learn more about the characters she has created at her website where they have their very own page. It will be updated from time to time to let you know what's going on with them. You can also find out who will be in the next book.

Crissy Smith loves to hear from readers. You can find contact information, website details and an author profile page at https://www.totallybound.com/

Home of Erotic Romance